Jury of Peers

City Stories

Dan Wallace

Wylisc Press
Silver Spring, MD

Published 2021 by Wylisc Press

Jury of Peers
City Stories
Dan Wallace

ISBN 9781735300603 Trade Paperback
ISBN 9781735300610 E-Book
6 x 9
195 pages
Publication Date: January 2021
Cover design by Molly A. Wallace

Wylisc Press
Silver Spring, MD 20901-1205
Inthewallacemanner.com

To Lucie
my Irish twin,
editor, reader,
and pal

Contents

Jury of Peers

At break time, Ken left the construction site and walked through the side door that lead to the school parking lot. The sun burned fiercely, but he couldn't get a good signal unless he left the shade of the eaves. He stepped out and hit speed dial.

"Hello?"

"Hi, Grace, it's me. How are you?"

Silence. "What do you want, Ken?"

"Okay," he said evenly, "enough with the pleasantries. I called to tell you I can't pick up the kids from school Friday."

"What? Why?"

"I have to go to Philly for jury duty."

"Oh, come on, Ken, jury duty? Give me a break. You're the only person in the world who can't get out of jury duty?"

"I already have, three times. They keep calling me back and I've pretty much run out of dead parents and broken legs."

"I don't get it, you don't even vote. And Philly? Why Philly?"

"It's federal duty."

"Oh. I suppose you pay some taxes. Well, what the heck am I supposed to do Friday? I can't leave work early again, they'll dock me, if they don't fire me. You keep pulling this shit, Ken."

"Grace, what can I do? It's just this Friday afternoon, I'll be there that night to get them. If it was anything else, I wouldn't be doing this."

"Yeah, sure, it's always just this one time, then another, and another. You make me sick, Ken, with your constant bullshit."

"Believe me, it's just this Friday. It's the last day, I've been going all last week and this week. I might even be able to make it Friday; if we don't get called for a case, they let us go for the day. I've been showing up to work for half days. If they let us off tomorrow, I can call you and pick Penny and Josh up just like always."

"But, if you don't, I have to walk into my boss's office and tell him that I have to leave suddenly? That's really well thought out, Ken, genius."

Ken pressed his lips together, then breathed, "Grace, what can I tell you? It's the Feds."

"And next time it'll be the terrorists. Well, forget it. If you can't make it on time Friday, then don't bother showing up at all."

"But I haven't seen them for two weeks, Grace—" but she had hung up.

Ken's face darkened even in the brilliant sunlight. He looked at the phone as if it was at fault, then moved to smash it on the pavement. But he held up. His fury turned cold, and he calmly hit redial. No answer. He paused, then hit it again.

"Hi, this 215-930-9734, a private residence . . . ."

Ken closed the phone and slipped it into his pocket as he headed back into the school.

Despite his troubles, Ken had found the jury duty to be pretty interesting. After passing through a security gate at the entrance to the federal court building, everyone was sent up to a big room with a hundred chairs. Tall, lean, and blond, and sporting a truck-driver's tan on his face and arms, he'd worn his only sports coat over his usual blue work shirt and jeans, a concession to what he imagined the dress code would be in federal court, like in church. He got over that soon enough, ditching the coat and allowing his blond stubble to grow for a few days before shaving it off, then starting over again.

On the first day, a clerk explained to them how it all worked. They were thanked for appearing and told that their service would last two weeks or the length of any trial upon which they might serve. They would be called by name and asked to report to a courtroom where a new jury would be chosen.

"The number of names called depends upon the case. If it's a fairly regular kind of case, 30 or 40 people might be called to find a jury of twelve plus one or two substitutes. If it's a big, high profile case, like that Peterson one out in California, they could empty the room and still not find twelve objective people."

"Is O.J. up again?" someone called out, and the room broke into laughter.

The clerk smiled, a very attractive Black woman dressed smartly in a black business suit and a violet shirt.

"As far as we know, a case involving Mr. Simpson has not been scheduled. But we do a few fairly well-publicized cases, which can test our capacity to find a jury. In all but a few, rare instances, we do seat a representative jury. Most cases last two to three days, some as many as five. If you find yourself on such a case, and it ends after a few days, you will need to return here to possibly be available for another case. If you aren't selected again, sometimes you are permitted to return home before the full two weeks have passed."

"Do any of the cases last longer than two weeks?"

She said, "Some do," and everyone groaned.

"Listen," she said, grimacing slightly, "some last for much longer. It all depends on what kind of case it is and how much evidence is to be presented. An investment fraud case tried here did not reach the jury for a month and a half. But, be thankful that you're not in Washington facing a big government scandal case. You could be sequestered in a hotel for the entire time."

She then explained the voir dire process, and how the attorneys were allowed to dismiss a certain number of potential jurors just because they didn't like their looks, nothing personal, and everyone laughed again. Also, she warned, the judge would ask each candidate if there was any reason they shouldn't serve on this case, whether they knew the defendant, the attorneys, like that.

"These questions are not to be answered frivolously," she said firmly, "Jury duty is not just something to get out of, it's a public service of vital importance to the fairness of our jurisprudence system. Voir dire means 'to tell the truth.' So, please answer honestly. Even if you don't, you'll find yourself right back in one of these chairs for the next case, one that you can't wriggle out of, and it could be a lot worse!"

They laughed again. Ken remembered going to his first voir dire, riding in the elevator with Pat Kennedy, a Black postal carrier, and some others. They went in, sat down, and the judge explained the case in which a postal worker was shot five times by a young man sitting in a car blocking his truck. When he went to complain, the young man shot him, three times in the front and twice in the back as he tried to run away. Miraculously, the postal worker had survived and would testify. The federal case hinged upon whether or not the postal worker, by leaving his truck, had been pursuing a personal folly.

"Mr. Kennedy, you feel that you cannot serve on this jury?"

"Yes, your honor," said Kennedy. "I work for the United States Postal Service and I believe that might prejudice me against the defendant."

"Thank you, Mr. Kennedy, you are dismissed from this case."

"I kill that little motherfucker, I break his fuckin' neck I see him in the street. I stick that gun up his ass!" yelled Kennedy as they rode back down to the second floor in the elevator. Ken smiled slightly as the others laughed. He had been dismissed summarily, no questions, no reasons given.

They straggled back to the waiting room to sit and talk or read. Most had found afternoons dragged, with little likelihood of another call to a trial. The talking helped.

Ken listened to Ed Muftee talk about the time he pulled someone out of a raging fire in a row house near his. "I got him out, all right, and got this burn on my arm."

He rolled his sleeve up to show a long, wide, nasty flash scar on his arm running from his wrist to his elbow. "I fell against a metal cabinet door. Couldn't see a damn thing from the smoke and all. I finally dropped to the floor and crawled forward, reaching ahead of me with my hand until I felt his leg. I dragged him out that way, out the front door and down the steps."

He sighed, "Of course, he didn't make it, but some people still said I was a hero. I don't see it if he didn't make it."

Ken looked him over, a quiet, light-skinned Black man, curly hair fading back from his brow. He looked like a nice guy, not assuming that defensive, fierce pose like Kennedy, who seemed just as nice when you talked to him.

"I'd call you a hero, Ed," said Ken. "It wasn't like your life was in any less danger because the guy died. You earned honor."

"Yeah," Muftee said quietly. "I still dream about it now and then."

Kennedy looked at Ken, and said, "You military, Pruitt?"

Ken glanced at him. "Yeah. Navy."

"Unhuh. How many fires you jumped into?" Kennedy asked.

Ken paused, then said, "What about you?"

"That's right, I was in the service, too, the Army, but no deep shit. Fort Belvoir, the motor pool, you know, Sergeant Bilko and all that. But, you, you saw some shit, right, some spooky stuff? I can tell just by the way you sit there, all catlike relaxed and shit."

Ken shrugged, "I was in the Seals."

Kennedy exploded laughter, "I told you, man! Hey, Muftee, don't mess with this one, he'll tear you up! He'll definitely tear you a new one. The Seals, huh? Shit, man, what'd you see, you into that Iraqi shit?"

"I retired a long time ago. I'm too old for that kind of stuff anymore."

"Oh, yeah," giggled Kennedy, "I buy that. Don't mess with him, Ed, he's a bad, baad man! Yessir, Mr. Pruitt, yessir."

"Hey, cut it out, will you, I'm just a carpenter now, that's all."

'Yeah, I'll bet you can swing a hammer!"

"Kennedy," Ken said, "shut up, will you?"

"You betcha, Mr. Pruitt, yessir. Get you some coffee?"

Ken feinted, and Kennedy flinched, almost choking with laughter.

"See how slow that was?" Ken said, and the three of them laughed.

This Friday morning, Ken was hardly relaxed. If he was lucky, he thought, maybe he could get through the morning fast enough to call Grace and salvage something out of this. Otherwise, he wouldn't see the kids for three weeks. Josh could be a foot taller by then and calling that asshole Grace dated his father.

He took his seat next to Ed Muftee and Kennedy and waited for the clerk to call the first case. Just then, Mary Roberts, a short, round woman sat down with them.

"You want to hear something cold-blooded," she said. "That young boy who shot the postman? He was sitting right next to me on the train, plain as you!"

"He ain't in custody?" Kennedy asked, amazed.

"No!" she said. "There he was, looking as slick as he could be in a beautiful, brand new suit. I swear he bought it for the trial."

The three of them joined in fast conversation, while Ken flipped open his cell phone to see if he had any messages. None. He started to dial when the clerk started talking. One by one, Kennedy, Muftee, and Mary Roberts were called, but not him. Most of the chairs were empty, now, on a Friday morning. The old lawyer rule seemed to apply, everyone wants to get home for the weekend. Ken did, too.

Kennedy, Muftee, and Mary Roberts came back in and sat down.

"A product liability case," Kennedy said. "Some guy went home, drank a couple of beers for lunch, then came back to work just in time to lop his finger off in a drill press. But the suit says it ain't his fault, it isn't his bosses' fault for not keepin' a safer workplace, it's the drill press manufacturer's fault. The damn thing was made in 1915! But, it's their fault, no matter."

They sat. Ed broke out a deck of cards to play gin with Kennedy. Mary put on some thick glasses and dove into the middle of a fat paperback, *Love's Knave* something.

Ken squirmed, checked his watch, then the big clock on the wall. Ten-thirty.

He twisted in his chair, then darted up and strode to the front desk.

"Excuse me, m'am, but it's getting late. Think they'll keep us much longer? It's Friday, and . . .."

"Maybe 'til noon," she said, smiling warmly. "If there's nothing by then, I'm pretty sure they'll let us all go home, thank God."

"Oh, that'd be great. Listen, I can't get a signal in here, do you think it would be okay for me to step outside quick and make a call?"

She looked both ways, then smiled, "Well, if you make it fast. You never know when they'll call."

"Okay, great, thanks so much."

He turned to leave, and the phone on her desk rang.

She picked it up, then looked at him, frowning sympathetically.

"Right," he murmured as he headed back to his chair.

"Oh," she said. She stood up. "Could I have everyone's attention. That was from Courtroom 16-A. I'm afraid they need all of you to go upstairs."

Ken's chin sunk into his own chest. Everyone.

"All of us?" cried Kennedy. "What the hell kind of case would need all of us up there?"

The suit looked them over, wearing a kindly expression. Ken couldn't recall seeing a collar whiter than the one sticking out of his jacket, which in itself was made of some soft, almost velvet-like material. The man in it was deeply tanned, and bald except for some strands of black hair moussed back against each side of his head.

"Have any of you heard of the Racketeer Influenced and Corrupt Organizations Act?" he asked. No one responded. "How about a

RICO case?"

"*Law and Order*, that's a Mob case, man, Tony Soprano."

The lawyer addressing them glanced down at a woman sitting at a table next to him, and she took a note.

"Yes, well, that's television, but this is the real thing. In front of you, today, is a federal indictment for conspiracy of Mr. Peter Innunzio, formerly Gabriele d'Annunzio until 1965. Also known as Pistol Pete, he is the current CEO of the Scarfo family, which has dominated organized crime in Philadelphia for 30 years."

"Hey," Ed whispered, nodding his head in the direction of the speaker, "he's the prosecutor. The way he looks, I thought he was the Bruce Cutler dude in this." Seeing puzzled looks, he said, "You know, the Mob mouthpiece."

"Ladies and gentlemen," the suit went on, "you are here to be considered as a juror in a Mafia trial."

Shit, thought Ken, the weekend is screwed.

The voir dire plodded on for the two hours left in the morning, and three more in the afternoon. Thirteen of the necessary 18 jurors had been selected. Trained to be infinitely patient, Ken drummed the back of the chair with his fingers until Kennedy glared at him. He switched to his thigh, which made no noise. One by one, Ed Muftee, Mary Roberts, and Pat Kennedy—surprise, his first name, thought Ken—were interviewed and dismissed without prejudice. Kennedy stood and patted him on the back as he left, "Hang in there, Pruitt, another hour or so, you' be on your way home for the weekend. Take care of yourself, man."

Too late, thought Ken.

The federal attorney called out, "Number 181."

Ken gazed at the cardboard square in his hand: 181. Finally.

He raised his hand and the attorney motioned to his counterpart, Peter Innunzio's lawyer. A short, round man with a florid complexion and graying hair, he spoke with a discernable accent, more New York than Philly. He, too, wore an expensive suit, charcoal gray, impeccably fitted. On his left pinky, he sported a gold class ring, nothing else.

"Mr. 181, I'm Earl McCarthy, counsel for Mr. Innunzio. How are you?"

"I'm fine," Ken said tersely.

"Yes, well, we all want to get home. Let me start by asking you if you've ever heard of the Mafia? Have you?"

"Sure. *The Godfather*, *Godfather II*, *III*, *Donnie Brasco*, all of them. Who hasn't?"

"Right, all very entertaining cinema. Do you think they were based in reality?"

"Do you mean do I think there's a Mob here? Sure, there's one everywhere in the world."

"You believe an Italian Cosa Nostra exists in China?"

"No," Ken said scornfully, "they have their own outfits. This isn't an ethnic thing."

"No, of course it isn't" said McCarthy. "Do you read the newspapers?"

Ken shook his head, "Not regularly. The sports page. Headlines, occasionally."

"Unhuh. Watch the news on TV?"

"Nope. *The History Channel*, though some people call it the Hitler Channel."

Those left in the room laughed weakly.

"Are you familiar in any way with the name Peter Innunzio?"

"No. I have heard of the Scarfo family, though," Ken said hopefully, "on *The History Channel.*"

"Unhuh. But not Mr. Innunzio. Nor the sobriquet 'Pistol Pete'?"

"Sobriquet? Is that something like AA?"

McCarthy laughed, "Thank you, that's all." He glanced at the federal attorney, then took his seat.

The federal attorney rose and approached the gallery. "My name is

Harry Lupino, the federal prosecutor in this case. It says in your form that you were in the Navy. Is that so?"

"Yes."

"Career?"

"I retired after nine years."

"Why nine, why not twenty?"

Ken shrugged, shifting uncomfortably. "Nine years means you don't have to be in the reserves. My wife wanted me out."

"I see, of course. But you were pretty much a career serviceman, is that right?"

"For nine years."

"That means that you believe in your country, correct? Defending your country?"

"I guess so, sure."

"Would you have given your life for your country?"

Ken raced back to drops in Bagdad, painting missile targets with a laser designator, decommissioning that sentry on his way back out into the desert to be picked up. He recalled rappelling into the Guatemalan jungle to stand black-leafed against a tree while rebel after rebel stole by, for nine hours until the mission was aborted, waiting another four before he could move.

"Sure," he said, "I guess."

"Then you believe in the principles that guide our country, the values? You know the difference between right and wrong, is that so?"

Ken pinched his lips, then said, "I suppose."

Lupino faced the judge and said, "Number 181 is acceptable to the prosecution, your Honor."

The judge turned to McCarthy, who half rose from his seat, "Mr. 181 is acceptable to the defense as well, your Honor."

Ken left the chamber, stunned. Instead of fretting, why hadn't he listened to the rest of them answer questions? He might have picked up on some key words that would have gotten him out. Now, he was relentlessly fucked.

They were to be sequestered and were told to get their affairs in order for a long stay, as much as six months. He'd lose his kids for forever.

"Hello?" Penny answered.

"Hi, Penny-for-Your-Thoughts. Daddy here." He pictured her lounging on the divan, watching the TV on mute while she talked, twirling her strawberry curls with her free hand, the same as her mothers, twirling them just the same way.

"Hi, Poppa, why couldn't you come get us this weekend? We miss you and we're bored."

"I know, I know, I couldn't help it. I'm downtown on jury duty. I'm going to be in a trial, and it looks like it's going to take a long time."

"Trial? What did you do? How long will you be in jail?"

He smiled, "No, I'm not going to jail, I didn't do anything. I'm on the jury, I'll be deciding whether this other guy committed a crime."

"Did he? What'd he do?"

"I don't know that, yet, I have to hear what everyone says, first. They say it's going to take a long time, like months."

"Oh, that's too bad, Daddy. Can you tell me about it when you pick us up?"

Ken grimaced silently. "That's why I'm calling, Sweets. I don't think I'll be able to pick you or Josh up anytime soon. They're keeping us in a hotel downtown while this goes on."

"Oh. That's not good."

"No," he said trailing off. They didn't speak for a time, he figuring that some show had caught her eye. "Okay, Sweet Stuff, I gotta go. Say hi to Josh for me, will you?"

"Sure, Daddy. I'll miss you, I love you."

"Yeah, me, too."

"Oh, and Daddy?" She paused, then said, "'ospital!" in a Cockney accent.

He laughed and repeated it back to her "'ospital.'"

Years ago in Pakistan he'd partnered up with a Brit Ranger who, whenever he saw him, would meet him with a balled-up fist and a lethal squint, and say "'ospital, mate, 'ospital!" Ken had brought it home with him to tease his kids, who would scurry away gleefully, laughing at an almost hysterical pitch. Now, it was Penny's greeting for him, Penny-for-Your-Thoughts.

"Six months? Well, that's it, Ken, that's enough. These kids have lived their entire lives with an absentee father. They're better off without one at all."

"Oh, come on Grace, this isn't my fault. I got picked for this, I didn't volunteer."

"I'm sure that's true, at least in your mind. But somehow you managed to be in the thick of it. Well, the kids don't need this and neither do I. While you're judging your Mafia boss I'll be filing for full custody."

"For Christ's sake, Grace!"

"I am, I'm going to do it—"

"On what grounds?"

"Desertion!"

"Oh, bullshit, that'll never fly!"

"Well, just you think so. While you're playing with your cops and robbers, think of what the judge will say when you don't even show up in court!"

"God damn it, Grace, why are you doing this? I love the kids, our kids."

"If you love them, you'll let me do this so that they can have a normal life."

"Oh, right, normal, like every other normal kid from divorced parents. Like you, for example."

She hung up. The case began.

Except for the first day, when they first saw Peter Innunzio, the case bored them to tears. Free on bail after surrendering his passport, he walked in with his lawyer and took his seat at the defendant's table. Innunzio wasn't particularly anything, Ken thought, not tall, not skinny or fat, in his early to mid-sixties, maybe, with undistinguished gray hair a little bit in need of a haircut. His skin was sallow, his eyes droopy with bags. He wore thick glasses, graduated apparently, since when he read anything, he looked down his nose. Ken noticed that his wrists were small, almost delicate. Occasionally, when he crossed his legs, Ken could see them, whiter than white, muscular calves, hair worn away by the brush of his pant legs. His suits looked to be of good quality, but old, as though they'd been hung in the closet for a long time without being worn. Just like many head men that Ken had seen in his day, Pistol Pete didn't look at all hard, which didn't mean a thing. He must be smart, at least smarter than his friends, and ruthless. But, right now, he struck him as more of an Uncle Innunzio, let's sing a Dean Martin song.

Days dragged on as the prosecutors took turns introducing evidence, long-winded tapes from wiretaps that sounded like guys on television talking in street code about this thing or that. The prosecutors then would swear in an expert witness, who would interpret the tape for the jury.

After which McCarthy would get up and cross-examine, trying to befuddle the witnesses into a mistake. While this went on, Ken inspected the large chamber, the exquisitely varnished wood paneling, the handsome ceramic tile floors, all a contrast to the stylized, faux sash windows that looked like they dated back to the 50s, *Twelve Angry Men*.

This jury wasn't like that, of course. They started with 18, but two claimed to be sick, and one begged off because of a family crisis. Ken had been toying with the idea of trying to get out, but just as he was ready to give it a shot, the family-crisis member cried. The judge let her go, then immediately turned to reprimand the rest of the jury about dodging their civic duty.

"Man, it's like he'd sic the IRS on us," Colin Brady moaned. He was in his 20s, single, and antsy about having to sit still for so long.

"He just might, pal, he just might." Another juror, Ira Leopold sat quietly most of the time unless he was expressing his skepticism about anything associated with the government. McCarthy must have picked Ira, Ken thought.

"If he let three people go, I can't see how he'd let anyone else," Bea Towe said, a slight woman with streaked blond hair. She was a grade school administrator from Tamaqua who worried about the time she was missing with her staff, her students, her family. Yet, her sense of civic duty pulled her the other way, too, Ken noted.

"I don't think any more of us are likely to get off the hook," he said to her. "We'll just have to tough it out."

He couldn't believe he was trying to console her when he felt almost frantic himself.

"She's doing what she can in court," Bobbie, his lawyer told him. "She's painted a pretty nasty picture of you, playing up the crazy Navy Seal PTSD aspect, you know? It's hard to refute when you can't make the court dates, and the judge hasn't been completely patient about rescheduling. You can't shake loose for one day?"

"No, I can't. They've got us all locked up for our own protection in an old hotel which I can't even name. They even told us they spot-check our cell calls, listening in to be sure that no one outside talks about the stupid trial. We're not supposed to ask anything, and you can't tell us anything. The judge has threatened to jail any of us who cross the line for contempt. You've got to tell the family court judge all of this. I mean, isn't there any professional courtesy extended here?"

"Not when it's Family Court versus the Feds."

"Well, shit, then."

A pause ensued, until Bobbie said, "Also, uh, she's showing up not alone."

"What? That asshole? He's with her?"

"He sits near her in the gallery. The judge can see that she has that kind of support."

"God damn it! Bobbie, what can I do?"

Again, silence. "Look, if she gets full custody, she still has to let you see your kids."

"She barely lets me see them now! What if she moves?"

"She won't move, Ken. Remember the asshole."

Ken sighed. "This sucks, Bobbie."

"I know, I know. There's another hearing next week. I'll let you know how it turns out."

Yeah, and how am I going to pay you? He asked himself this after she'd hung up. How long are you going to do this for free?

During recesses, Ken spent most of his time with Ira, Colin, and Bea. He knew the other eight jurors by name and profession, the tinker, the tailor, and all that. But, mostly, he lived with those he'd first met. White-haired Ira had worked at the newspapers until he retired ten years ago. "First hot type, then cold type," he said, "all at *The Inquirer*, the best newspaper in the business, those cheap bastards."

Colin had majored in dance and now delivered pizza at night so that he could audition during the day. "That's why I'm here, I guess," he said forlornly. "It's easier to impose on those without fixed incomes."

"Most of us here have jobs," said Bea.

"Yeah, but you get the summer off."

"I still have to work in the summer. We have summer school. Besides, I have a family."

Bea had a three-year-old son and a husband who, from what Ken overheard on their phone conversations, wasn't completely supportive of his wife when he learned that the boy had another six-months of potty training in front of him. After hanging up on the phone at the six-week mark, she cried silently. Ken hugged her, and said, "As bad as it is for you, Bea, it could be worse."

She sobbed a laugh, "Yeah, but it could get that way. Or are you telling me it's going to get better?"

"Well," he said, "it could be worse for now."

They stood in an alley in back of the courthouse, the only place where they could get good signals on their cells. Other jury members smoked, while the guards stood by. A corps had been assigned to babysit them, take them back and forth from the courtroom to their deliberation room, then drive them to their hotel at the end of each day. In conversation, Ken had mentioned that he'd been in Special Forces, and Colin told one of them, Joe Fagley. A red-faced dreamer in his early 30s and far removed from his sporting days, Joe immediately asked Ken to tell some war stories. At first, Ken demurred, until he thought that he might be able to work a few extras out of the relationship. So, he told Joe a few, watching the eyes of the heavy guard go puppy-dog.

Hugging Bea wasn't bad, Ken thought. He wondered just how lonely they all would get, stuck here as they were, when his cell phone went off. He pulled himself reluctantly away from Bea, stepped away with a smile, and flipped it open.

"Yeah," he said.

"Ken Pruitt."

"Right, that's me, who's this?"

"'ospital,' Pruitt," without any trace of a Cockney accent.

Ken's smile faded into a frown. "Who is this?"

"A friend, maybe. Go to the office where you pick up your mail. There's a bench right outside the door. You'll see a guy holding a brown paper bag on it. Have lunch on us." He hung up.

Ken turned off his phone and said to Joe, "Joe, I forgot to pick up my mail."

"Well, you better hurry," he said. "The judge will be calling you all back in a couple of minutes."

Ken speed-walked to the front of the large building, past a phalanx of elevators to an administrative office at the right corner near the X-ray machines. Even before he got there, he could see an old Black guy in worn-out clothes clutching a bag in his lap. As soon as he saw Ken approach, he propped the bag against the arm of the wooden bench, stood up, and left. Ken picked up the bag and looked inside. A salami sandwich, chips, an apple, and a large, chocolate chip cookie. A cell phone, prepaid, one that couldn't be monitored since the guards didn't know about it.

He opened it and found a sticky inside with a number on it, and beneath that, "After five."

Walking toward the elevators, he dumped the bag into a trash bin, and pocketed the cell.

The same voice answered, "Yeah."

"What are you doing with my daughter?" Ken said, barely keeping his voice even, resisting the overwhelming desire to rain epithets on the unknown caller. The horror of sitting through the drone of the testimony for three hours had been enough to wear him out, but adrenaline pushed through him now. Once released by the judge, he'd pounded down the stairs to the back of the courthouse, moving to a far corner away from any other jurors or guards.

"Nothing, Ken, nothing at all. She's perfectly safe, believe me, she's fine. We didn't do nothing that the government doesn't do. Even to civilians these days, as it turns out."

Wiretap. They'd wiretapped the phones in his home, Grace's home.

"What do you want?"

"A service, Ken, a very simple, easy service, one that will make sure that your daughter and your whole family stays safe and healthy. And you, too, Ken."

"What do you want?"

"Nothing for free, of course. If you do this service, we'll make it worth your while. Say, ten. Ten for school for your kids."

"Last time: what do you want?"

"Simple. Just say no."

The line clicked off. Ken dialed the number again, but no one answered. He waited until a disembodied voice informed him that the phone had transferred him to voice mail, but that this customer did not possess voice mail, Goodbye.

Dinner never excited the jurors much, but Ken seemed to eat in a trance, as though the meal tasted more like cardboard than ever before. Bea leaned over and said, "Are you all right, Ken?"

He shifted his eyes to her. "I'm fine. Everything is just fine."

He called Grace right afterward.

"How are you?"

"I'm all right. Surprised that you called." She sounded unsettled, maybe by his tone, he thought. He tried to lighten up the mood, "I'm bored. Our bent-nosed defendant is, basically, boring."

"Oh. I thought it'd be more interesting, I guess."

"Yeah, how are the kids?" Again, he tried to keep anxiety out of his voice.

"They're fine," she said in a measured tone. She hesitated, then said, "You haven't heard, have you?"

"Heard what?"

"Your lawyer hasn't spoken to you?"

His stomach fell as far as it could, the same as when he'd received the anonymous phone call.

"About what?"

"Ken," she said, "the judge has granted me full custody."

He was wrong; his stomach hit a new bottom.

"Aw, Grace."

"I'm sorry, Ken," she said almost in a sob, hurriedly, "but it's for their own good. You're never around, they need a full-time father. The uncertainty undermines their confidence, Ken. They need stability."

"For God's sake, Grace, not more *Doctor Phil.* I see them when I can, and they seem to be fine with it."

"That's how much you know. You don't see them, how they look when you miss a soccer game or an awards ceremony at school."

"I work, Grace, to pay you support. Those awards always get given out in the morning. If you transferred them into the school I'm working on now, maybe I could see them on my breaks!"

Silence, until she said in a stone-cold voice, "That just isn't good enough, Ken, it doesn't even make sense."

More silence, until he said, "I suppose I'll never see them now."

"Of course you will, but on a different schedule."

"Unhuh, and what if you decide to move? Then what?"

"I'm not planning to move."

"Yeah, but what if you do? What's keeping you here?" No answer, and he gradually figured it out. "I get it; the asshole. You're not planning to move while he's in the picture. I suppose he's the perfect father that I'm not, huh?"

"Good night, Ken," she said.

"Maybe it's in my interest that you do move," he said, but she was gone.

Damn that Bobbie. And now he had to deal with Pistol Pete and his friends.

The next morning, the testimony droned on, the circumstantial evidence mounted, and the jurors endured. During a short recess, Bea came to him and asked, "You feeling okay? You look like you slept standing up."

He smiled and said, "I'm okay. I'm sort of sorting things out. And I think they're coming together."

No other call came through to him, either on his phone or on the lunch bag cell. He had spent all night up, cycling through the misery of his life, the fear, and wild ideas for solving all of his problems. To break the thoughts looping through him, he hit the floor and pushed out 50 push-ups, collapsing airless and embarrassed at his poor condition. This sitting all day for months was sacking his strength. As he sat and thought about his options, he realized that he needed to get in shape for whatever might come.

"Joe, did I ever tell you about the bar fight in Mission, California?" He watched Joe's eyes light up as he continued. "A pal of mine Dick Wise and I were dredging for beers and babes there, on the wrong side of town. We found a whole lot of the first and none of the last until we entered this one bar where there were a few sweethearts. So, we walk in, order a beer, and sidle up to a table where a couple of rough-looking cuties were sitting. In our beer haze, what we hadn't noticed was that this was a biker bar."

Joe emitted a nervous laugh and leaned forward in anticipation.

"I start making time with this one honey when the biggest mountain shaped like a man walks up, grabs my arm, and twirls me around. 'Hey, man,' he yells, 'what the hell do you think you're doing with my old lady?'

"It was then that Dick and I noticed that twenty other guys, all wearing this dude's colors, were closing in on us, waiting for him to say jump and how high. I'm thinking then, 'Oh shit, we're dead,' when Dick flashes by me fast as hell. He always was faster than light.

"And this giant biker dude starts screaming at the top of his lungs, standing there with one of his eyes hanging out of its socket. He's screaming, until Dick shouts 'Hey!' and the guy stops yowling all at once.

"'If you take him to the hospital right now,' Dick says, 'they can put it back in the socket.' Well, I'm telling you, they fell all over each other saying, 'Yessir, that's a good idea, thank you sir, we'll get him there right away.' And that's what they did; we walked right on out of there ourselves at the same time, no worries."

Joe's mouth sagged, fixed open. "You're shittin' me," he said breathlessly.

"No, I'm not. And one of these days, I'll show you how to do it. Now, I need some exercise, Joe. You know, this sitting around is wearing on a guy like me."

"Sure, I understand."

"I knew you would. So, I thought running the hotel stairs would be good, maybe after dinner or in the morning. Think you could help me keep the stairwells open while I do that?"

"You bet Ken," he said, then, "In fact, I might even join you."

"Now, that's all right, Joe, you've got a job to do. But, when this is all over, maybe we can get together to work out."

"Aw yeah, man!"

"Okay, then."

After a week, he felt more like his old self, nowhere near operations level, but good enough for anything that might come along. The phone hadn't rung, but it didn't matter. Nothing would happen to Grace or the kids while the trial went on, nothing until he'd spoken to Innunzio's friend again. So, he trained, and he waited.

Two weeks later, the new cell rang.

"Hello, Ken. Have you considered our offer?"

The voice sounded detached, as though this was a routine sales call. Considering Pistol Pete's track record in court and that of his associates, maybe it was routine.

"You have a name?"

"Not on the phone I don't. Anyway, all you got to say is yes or no. And it better not be no."

"Okay, I'll give you a name: how about Louie? You like Louie?"

A pause, and the voice somewhat nasally said, "How'd you know my name was Lou?"

"Why, I tossed up a bunch of wise-guy names in my head and came up with Louie," Ken said. "Louie's a wise-guy name, isn't it, Louie?"

"You can call me anything you want, asshole, as long as you answer the question right. What's it gonna be?"

"Listen, Louie, I appreciate the offer, and I've thought it over, and I have a counteroffer."

"A counteroffer? What do you mean a counteroffer? This isn't *Let's Make a Deal*, motherfucker. If you mean more money, you're lucky you're gettin' fuck-all. Keep talkin', Ken, and I can arrange that."

"No, no, the money's okay for what I have in mind," Ken said, starting to feel giddy this deep into it.

"And what do you have in mind, shithead?"

"A job. I want you to give me a job."

The cell sounded like it had gone dead. "Can you hear me, Louie?"

"I can hear you. What are you, addicted?"

"No, I need a job."

"You better start getting serious, Ken, or somebody could get hurt."

"No, no, listen to me, Louie, listen carefully. You give me a job, I deliver Mr. Innunzio back home as soon as I get the opportunity. Simple as that. Consider the ten thousand payment for the job. And, if you like my work, I'm happy to entertain more work."

"What're you, nuts? This call is over." He hung up.

Shit, thought Ken. He redialed the original number and got the voicemail/no voicemail message again. Now what?

The trial continued, and since he knew what his vote would be, Ken ignored it and started to observe the other jurors. Another week passed until he saw who it was. Bea.

After the morning break, she came back to the jury's room appearing as though she'd suffered an acute attack of anemia. Clutched in her hand was a brown paper bag.

Ken went over to her and gently grabbed the bag. "Come with me," he said.

He led her into the hall, stopped to whisper to Joey, who smiled knowingly. Then, he led her into the men's room with Joey outside the door.

"What, what are you doing, give me back that bag, I need it." She stuttered, "I'm hungry, Ken," as she grabbed for it.

"Bea," he said, holding it away. He turned it upside down over the trash bin. The sandwich, fruit, chips, and cookie tumbled into the bin, but he snatched the cell phone out of the air before it followed them.

"I know, Bea," he said. "The same thing happened to me. The night you saw me look like death warmed over, that's when it happened."

She started crying, heaving uncontrollably, slipping to the floor.

Ken leaned over and patted her back, "Don't cry, Bea, I've got this. Nothing's going to happen."

"He played a tape of him saying he missed me, he missed Mommy!"

"Don't, Bea. Don't worry, your boy and your husband will be safe, I guarantee it."

"How?" she cried, "what can you do to save them?"

"Nothing. Except, I can make sure it's me, not you or the others."

"You? Why is that a good solution? You have a family, too."

He was moved. In her worst nightmare, she could worry about his family.

"To tell you the truth, it's not much my family anymore. Anyway, I'll take care of it, and them, and no one's going to get hurt."

"How can you be so sure?"

He smiled.

At the end of the day, he slipped out to the back of the courthouse with Bea's new cell. He snapped it open and dialed the number, a new one, of course.

"Hello, Bea." The same nasal tone.

"Hello, Louie, how've you been? Miss me?"

"Who the . . . how'd you get this number?"

"I got her phone, too, dickhead. Who do you think you're dealing with, some asshole?"

"You just got yourself some problems, Sailor Boy. Oh, yeah, I know who you are, Swabby, Mr. Fix-It, and you just walked into it."

"Wrong, Louie, and don't hang up. If you send another phone to another juror, I'll be on the other end. See, I'm here, and you're there, and there isn't a goddamn thing you can do about it, get me?"

A moment passed. "Shit!"

"Right, now listen to me. You're supposed to be handling this for, I don't know, one of your bosses, McCarthy, maybe Pistol Pete himself."

"That's Mr. Innunzio to you, and he would never have anything to do with something like this."

"Yeah, Mr. Innunzio. And you've screwed it up, Louie, your jury has run away, just like in the movie."

"Bullshit. I'll get somebody and you won't be able to stop me."

"Oh, you don't know me that well, Louie. But, don't worry, I'm not in this to make you look bad. I was serious about a job, a certain kind of job."

"What are you talking about?"

"Oh, you must have something I can do, something wet that you need cleaned up."

Ken waited for an answer.

"You must watch too much television. You need to get back on your meds, pal."

"You said that before, Louie, but I have very unique skills, believe me. Tell you what, I'll do it on the cuff. You pay me after I've completed my work."

"I need to get off this phone."

"Sure, Louie, let's not talk about it now. I'll meet you somewhere to discuss my counter-offer."

"Are you kidding me? How you going to get out? They got you locked up!"

"Oh, I can get out, Louie, no worry about that. It'll be part of my demonstration, part of the test. I show up, and you give me a job. If I don't show up, you move on. What have you got to lose from that?"

Again, a pause. "Give me an address, Louie, and I'll come see you. We'll talk. Just give me an address."

Ken waited. "Go get a lunch bag tomorrow. Call the number for directions."

The cell went dead. Ken smiled to himself.

Joe didn't work the night shift, but a good friend of his did. Ken mentioned to Joe that he and Bea wanted time alone, so that he should tell his friend not to do too close a bed check in either room. Joe smiled, and said, Sure, he understood. It wasn't the first time it happened during a long, dragged-out trial.

At nine, Ken knocked on Bea's door. She let him in and he gave her a quick hug, then passed through her window and rambled down the fire escape. He headed west two blocks to a bus stop at Market Street where he caught the 127 South on 7th Street. The bus took the I-95 ramp north for ten minutes, then pulled off at the Cottman Street exit, and wended its way through to Hegerman, then Princeton.

Ken left the bus at Princeton and walked two more blocks to a side street, Baron. He walked down until he found a small deli, its name announced on a grimy green awning, Mickey's Deli Sandwiches. He stepped inside.

It wasn't big, two rows of tables on the side walls separated by little more than a body's width, a counter in the back for ordering. The walls were a bright orange, the tables were linoleum and chrome, and signs hand-written in faded black magic marker announced the deli's policies: No shoes, No food; No Seating without Ordering; The Management Reserves the Right to Deny Service to Any Customer.

One man sat at the second table in on the right. Graying and in his fifties, he sat reading the paper. In the back, two young men worked making sandwiches and pizzas.

Ken glanced over his shoulder, then moved closer to the seated man.

"Where's your order?" he asked.

He looked up from his paper. Folding it, he rose and said, "Wait here." He walked back behind the counter. Ken stepped back near the door and waited.

A young man wearing an open, double-breasted jacket and no tie emerged from the back. Loose-limbed, he walked slowly toward Ken. When he was two yards away, Ken said, "You must be Louie."

He smiled, a slender, dark-haired man, maybe 30, tan and good-looking.

"That's right, Sailor, I'm Lou. How'd you know?"

Ken laughed, "Just a lucky guess. Shit, what a stereotype."

Lou frowned, then said, "You're not. I have to admit, I'm surprised you showed up."

"In so many ways, I'm sure."

Lou smiled, "Not that way. I'm impressed. Why don't you sit down, we'll talk. I'll get you a sandwich, anything you like. What do you want to drink?"

Ken shook his head, "This isn't going to take that long."

The gray-haired guy came back from behind the counter and sat at an end table and unfolded his newspaper. Just then the door opened, forcing Ken to move closer in to the middle of the room. The man, big, strolled past him to the counter to order.

"Look, what can I tell you? We'll raise the ante to 20 grand, how's that? We don't want any hassles with you, just this simple thing. Why do you have to go and complicate it?"

"I need a job. I'm bored and I need to make more money. Surely you have someone who you'd rather was somewhere else? I can help you with that."

Lou shook his head, "You're just nuts, aren't you? You wearing a wire?"

Ken pulled up his t-shirt.

"Ah, that don't mean shit. But I'm not that interested in conducting a cavity search."

"Louie, you don't have to say anything more. Just give me a name and an address. I'll do the rest. I'll even work for you on the cuff, for the original ten as an act of faith. I'm interested in a long-term association, a new career. Just give me a name and address, and we'll be in business. And, think of it this way; if I do this for you, you'll not only have a valuable new resource, untraceable, you'll also have enough leverage on me to be sure that I'll do that other little thing for you when the time comes. Just give me a name and address. What have you got to lose?"

Lou turned to the man reading the paper. He looked at Lou, shrugged, then returned to his reading. At the counter, the big man received his order in a brown paper bag and turned to leave.

Lou faced Ken. He reached into his suit pocket and pulled out a slip of paper and handed it to him. "See what you can do with this."

Ken grinned. "You've made a wise decision, Louie," he said, as he opened the slip.

"It's Lou."

The slip was blank. Without looking up, Ken slid between the table and chair on his right, ending in a crouch, just missing a crack on his head from the wide arc of the big man's brown bag. He shoved the table into Lou as he stepped behind the extended arm of the big man and formed a stiff hook with his left index and middle fingers. Grabbing the big man's throat with his right hand, Ken plucked out one of his eyes with his left.

The man screamed, dropping the brown bag to cover his face with both hands. The bag landed on the floor with a thud. Still holding his throat, Ken groped inside the man's jacket, pulled out a gun and aimed it at Lou on the floor, then at the gray-haired man in the back.

Both of them stared with their mouths hanging open, only thinking to cover themselves with their hands in turn when Ken drew down on each of them, back and forth.

He pushed the big man back slowly to sit on the left table, then said, "If you take him to the hospital right now, they probably can put the eye back in."

Completely astonished, Lou almost forgot to keep his hands up. Glancing to make sure that the gray guy wasn't moving, Ken slipped over to Lou onto one knee and put the barrel of the gun, a Glock nine, up against his temple.

"I should send you to the morgue, motherfucker, threatening my kid."

Stark panic fled across Lou's face, until Ken said, "But I need a job, Lou." He stood up.

"Get me a name and address, and we can work together."

The trial could be winding down, he thought. The prosecutors had piled up a ton of evidence, but apparently this was only the background stuff. The jurors weren't allowed to read newspapers, but nobody could control the rumor mill. Apparently, lead P.A. Lupino had a star witness that could lay a murder directly at Pistol Pete's feet. When this happened, the guards murmured, the defense wouldn't have much to say.

"God, when will they put the guy in the box?" Colin wailed. "I've got to see the end of this soon or my life will be over."

"Don't be too sure this star witness will sink Innunzio," Ira said, shaking his finger. "Air-tight cases frequently have a way of leaking air."

Colin groaned, but Ken's ears pricked up. He looked at Ira hard, then waited until he could corner him alone.

"They got to you, huh, Ira?"

"What do you mean?"

"The phone call, the lunch bag?"

Ira's eyes flashed. Then, he relaxed. "The sandwich was good, the cookie stale."

"Did you call them back?"

"I did. I told them to go fuck themselves. How can they hurt me, those schmucks? My wife's dead, I got no kids and I hate everybody. Hah!"

Ken laughed, "Too bad, Ira, I like you."

Ira huffed, "Huh," then said, "They got hold of you, too?"

Ken nodded, "I think they'll go after all of us if they can. You know, why take a chance? They only need one vote, but why not three, or twelve?"

"Yeah," Ira said, rubbing his beard.

"But don't worry about it. I've found a way to make sure we don't have to worry."

"Okay," Ira said skeptically.

Ken called on Ira's phone. When he heard him answer, he smiled, but resisted the temptation. "Hello, Lou. How's your friend's eye? Twenty-twenty?"

"You shit, why didn't you tell me you were a Seal?"

He didn't answer, saying instead, "What'd I tell you about going after other jurors? I hear Ira told you to go fuck yourself."

"That old dick, so what?"

"So, I told you, I have them all sewn up. They've been persuaded to follow my lead. Understand?"

"Okay, okay."

"Now, let's get down to it. If you want that little thing done, you need to get me a name and address quick. I hear the prosecution is getting ready for the big finish."

Silence. "You hear me, Lou?"

"Yeah, I hear you. Okay. It'll be in the mail."

"The mail? Isn't that a bit chancy?"

"They don't open your mail, it's against the law. For Chrissake, you're not al-Qaeda or anything."

"Right. Okay, the mail."

Buddy Stanfield, a north Philly address; according to Wikipedia, he was a small-time dealer in the Solito family, Pistol Pete's main competition. Al (Umberto) Solito was thought to be responsible for dropping the dime on Pete by way of Buddy. Buddy tipped the Feds off about the star witness, Jerry Abbruzzese, who had been caught red-handed transporting narcotics and weapons across the New Jersey state line. With the new gun laws, Abbruzzese could be facing life in prison, unless he rolled on Innunzio. Abbruzzese was third in the family and knew everything. Apparently, Lou—Lou Cuscinetto—felt that a message needed to be sent, starting with Buddy Stanfield.

The first night, Ken waited outside the furniture shop where Buddy managed his dealers. Sitting in a parked car across the street, he waited for Buddy to leave at the end of his workday, three in the morning. He came out smoking a cigar, all three hundred pounds of him. He looked much bigger than the Wikipedia photo, and older. Buddy and two other guys talked in front of the shop for another 20 minutes. They separated at last, and Buddy climbed into a new Lexus SUV, alone. Ken shook his head at the arrogance.

The next evening, Buddy climbed into the Lexus where Ken, hiding in the back seat, wrung his neck.

"Well done, Ken. We're impressed. You are a useful guy."

"And I'm all yours, now, Lou."

"Absolutely. And how can I get you what's yours?"

"Mail it to me. They can't open it, remember?"

"Of course. And the other little thing will be taken care of?"

"Oh, yeah. That could be a problem, Lou."

Again, silence pressed down. "What do you mean?"

"I mean that with the P.A.s' star witness out there, our friend won't ever be safe. I can perform that little service that we've discussed, I can get my friends here to do what you want. But that doesn't mean that the P.A. or the judge won't smell a rat. The judge could throw out the whole thing, and you'd be back at square one with an entirely new jury."

"Shit," said Lou.

"Right," said Ken. "But there's another way to make this all go away forever."

"Yeah?"

"Yeah. Can you meet tonight to discuss it?"

"Okay, sure," said Lou, "for dinner. I owe you that much. Salvatore's Ristorante in the same neighborhood."

"I'll find it," said Ken.

Salvatore's Ristorante evoked old Italia, but lushly, with maroon velveteen-covered walls and thick linen tablecloths. The silver shone gold from age, and the hand-painted settings displayed gorgeous pastel scenes of city life, rural life, and robin-egg blue seas in the old country.

When Ken walked in, Lou stood to greet him, extending his hand to shake Ken's while patting him on the arm.

"Hi ya, Kenny, good to see you, or do you want me to call you just Ken?"

Ken laughed, "Whatever you want, Lou. I work for you, now."

"Nah, it's a business arrangement, see? We didn't know how valuable you are. We're going to have plenty for you to do when all this shit is over, believe me. See, even Georgy doesn't hold a grudge, do you Georgy?"

The big man had been sitting at a table in the back, the outsized white pad taped over his right eye seeming to bounce light off of his deeply tanned skin.

"Naw, Mr. Pruitt," he said, "just a misunderstanding. I know you had to do what you did, and the doctors say my eye will be as good as new."

He reached his hand out to Ken, who said, "Yeah, sorry Georgy, I didn't have much choice, I didn't want to hurt you permanently."

Georgy's eyes turned steely, and his grip suddenly came close to crushing Ken's hand. Ken readied his left, but Georgy let go and returned to his table.

"Sit, sit, let's eat."

They sat and ate incredibly delicious Italian dishes, a five-course meal. Ken had never eaten so well, and it was difficult to pace himself to ensure that he could move if necessary. Lou offered wine, but Ken declined, which genuinely seemed to disappoint his host. Finally, dessert and cappuccino were served.

Ken pushed back in his seat, full but not uncomfortable, and alert.

Lou paused, then said, "I've got something for you."

He pulled out a yellow envelope and pushed it across the table. Ken opened and peeked inside. U.S. bills.

"Thanks, Lou."

"Count it."

"That's okay, I know it's all there."

Lou shook his head, "There's more. A little bonus on account of how clean you work. As I said before, very impressive."

Ken nodded his head.

"So, what's this other idea you got for handling our situation?"

Ken said, "Jerry Abbruzzese."

A somber cast immediately fell across Lou's face. "What about that shit-bird rat?"

"I can take care of him for you."

Lou laughed, and Georgy joined in. Lou looked at Georgy and they both laughed hard, brittle laughs into each other's face, as though it was some kind of competition.

"Are you nuts? They got that prick hidden in a deeper hole than they got you guys, and we don't even know where that is."

Ken shook his head, "I have the run of the courthouse. The guards love me, they love hearing how I swung from a Blackbird into Baghdad and cut the throats of those terrorist pricks. They fall all over each other showing me around, how tough they can be when the bad guys are brought in for trial. I know exactly where they're going to hold Abbruzzese. All I need to know is the time they'll bring him to the courthouse and the day, and I can find that out from the guards, too."

Lou grimaced, shaking his head. "How sure are you, Kenny?"

"How sure were you that I couldn't do what I've done? You want the Abbruzzese problem to go away for good, this is the only way."

Lou thoughtfully nodded his head. "Okay."

"It'll cost you. Plenty. And up front."

Unhappy again, Lou said, "How much?"

"Three million."

"You're kidding. You're out of your mind."

"Innunzio's freedom isn't worth three million? He'll be happy to hear that."

Lou rolled his eyes. "Come on."

"Lou, don't ask me, ask him. See what he thinks."

Lou pouted. "If he does say yes, how do I get you the money? I can't give all that to you in a business envelope."

Ken laughed, "Laundry bag. No, I'll let you know what to do. Just, you better find out soon, because this case has been dragging on for too long. Lupino's got to be thinking about springing his star witness soon."

Lou nodded.

"Well, thanks for dinner and the present," he said, patting his pocket. He stood, and said, "Keep an eye out, Georgy," and left, Georgy glowering at him all the way out the door.

He climbed through Bea's window, and saw her drowsing on her bed. He tiptoed to the door, but she woke up. "How's it going?"

"Good. Things are pretty much under control. Tomorrow's Saturday and I have to go to the library again. So, I'll need you to tell Joe that we want another nooner, if you're up for it."

"Sure," she said, "I love sex, even if it's imaginary."

"Hey, don't get me started," he said as he slipped out, hearing the tinkling chime of her laughter fade as he closed the door.

You can Google anything, he thought, the Mob, offshore bank accounts, anything.

The end of the fourth month of the trial was closing in, a month since his first call from Lou Cuscinetto, and a week since their dinner. Lupino and his clones droned on about narcotics, prostitution, gambling, money laundering, larceny, extortion, assault, conspiracy—did he forget to mention battery? Ken crossed his legs, patiently not listening. He gazed at Peter "Pistol Pete" Innunzio and wondered what he was thinking. Was the gardener taking good care of his yard without his direction? Was he thinking about lunch? Did he want someone to take care of Al Solito for all of this trouble? Or was he thinking about a vacation in the old country? Surely, he wasn't thinking about transporting stolen goods across state lines.

Innunzio had a lived-in face, all rivers of wrinkles and crags. He'd gone through so much, Ken thought, and had made it this far. Sometimes, good things happen to bad people.

Lou called him at lunch time.

"It's a deal. But, half up front. You'll get the rest when it's done."

Ken paused, then said, "All right, good. Take down these numbers." He read off four sets, and a telephone number. "Transfer a half million into the first account, and half a million into the second. Split the remaining half million between the other two."

"You think ahead, don't you, Kenny."

"You bet, Lou, and you better transfer the money today. This trial is heating up fast. I need to know that the money's there before I do anything."

"Today? It's going to take time to get that kind of dough!"

"You gave me the go-ahead, which means the money's available.

You don't want Innunzio to find out that you've blown the whole thing by dragging your heels, do you, Louie?"

"Jesus, you're a mean prick."

"Yes I am, just what you need."

"And it's Lou."

"Sure it is. Get the money, Lou."

He checked the accounts after dinner and the money was all there. He breathed in and out deeply. The money was there.

"I have to go out tonight and I don't know how soon I'll be back. Probably early morning."

"Where are you going? Not to meet with them again?"

"No, no, that part's done. This may be the last time I have to go anywhere, but it has to be tonight. Can you cover for me one more time?"

Bea pressed her lips together, and a strand of fine blond hair caught in the corner of her mouth. She said, "Okay, okay. Maybe it'd be nice if for once I wasn't lying about you being here."

"Oh, Bea, don't. It's okay for me to torture myself daydreaming, but you have your boy, your husband back home to think about. Don't."

She dropped her head. "Yeah, I miss them so much."

"Well, this is almost over. Believe me, we're all going home soon."

He hugged her quickly, then slipped out the window early, taking his chances that one of the guards wouldn't see him. He had a long way to go, and he couldn't waste time.

He located the parking deck and breezed past the attendant's booth up the stairs three flights to the monthly rental area. There, he found Ira's car parked, dusty from a long stay. Ken unlocked the door and slipped in behind the wheel. Inserting key into the ignition, he suddenly felt a stark pang of fear flash through him wondering if it would start. Head down, he turned the key. The engine coughed, then roared to life. He sighed as he sat up. Enough gas, too.

He pulled out of the garage and headed for I-676 north to 76 and up the Schuykill Expressway to 476. He got off on Route 1 West and drove to Media.

From a distance, the house looked the same, white clapboard, scrubby lawn, the old garage in the back that had been his workshop. Closer up, he could see that someone had been working on the outside of the house. The shutters had been repainted, the flashing had been replaced on the front door, the driveway had been resealed. Evidence of the asshole, he thought. At least his car wasn't in the driveway. It was a school night, however, so Grace was sure to be home with the kids. More luck.

He parked down the street under a tree and walked back, slipping past one side of the house into the back yard. Gently, he tapped on the screen door.

The light flicked on and he could see Grace silhouetted against the door, peering out with her hand held to her forehead like an old Indian statue. A beat passed.

She opened the inside door and talked through the screen.

"Ken, what are doing here?"

"I'm here to see you, Grace." She stood leaning against the screen, standing on one leg while resting the other behind her. Her red hair fell just to her jaw line, curving toward him in two points at the end of a stylish page boy. Her skin still possessed that pinkish cast, so fair that a full summer of sunlight added just the slightest brown to her complexion. Her eyes were still green gems, too, he thought, and a slight ache rippled through him at the loss.

"I thought you were in that trial. You're not supposed to be here, are you?"

"No."

"Then, why are you here? I'm a little scared, Ken. Could you leave please?"

"I can't, Grace, I need to talk to you."

"Ken, I don't want to call the police."

"Please don't, Grace, I just need to talk to you for a short time, then I'll leave. I promise. Just let me in for ten minutes, ten minutes and I'll go."

She hesitated.

"Grace, in all that we've been through, I've never hurt you, I never wanted to. But this is really important, you have to believe me. You, the kids being safe, depend upon what I have to tell you."

Again, she hesitated. Then, she unlatched the door and let him in.

She gestured to a seat at the kitchen table and backed away to lean against the counter near the hallway. "Please make this not a mistake," she said to no one.

"It's not, believe me."

He sat, taking in the kitchen, which looked the same for the most part and completely different, too. The refrigerator was covered with photos and things from school that he'd never seen. She had some new plants on the windowsill above the sink, too. He remembered when they'd first separated, and the shock he'd had a year later when they met with their lawyers to sign the divorce papers. She was wearing a new winter coat, a stylish yellow parka with a fur collar, as if to show unthinkingly that her life had continued on while he was still stuck in the same misery. He felt that way now.

"What's so important, Ken?"

"How are the kids, are they asleep?"

"They're fine, and yes, they're in bed. What's the big emergency that has you sneaking out of a federal courtroom?"

"A hotel, actually. They have us penned up in a hotel."

"Fine, a hotel. What do you want?"

He winced, then forced himself to ignore it. "You know this case? It's a Mafia case?"

"Sure, it was in all the papers, on TV for a while. It's lasted so long, it's on the back pages, now. But I remember it, sure."

"Okay, it's about this. This guy Innunzio is up for murder."

And he told her everything, even about "'ospital," so that she knew it was real and serious. As he went on, she drew slowly toward him, and sat down at the table.

"Oh my God, they tapped my phone? Oh my God, what'll we do? My God!" She started to shake, "The kids!" she said, about to cry, and he grabbed her hand.

"Grace, don't. Don't worry. I'm going to take care of it. I'm going to get you all out of this."

"Out of this?" she cried. "How did you get us into it?"

The irrationality of the question seared him. "I was put on this jury!"

"Well, why didn't you get off the goddamn jury? Why didn't you lie, say you were sick or something? Why didn't you stay out of it?"

He shook his head, "I don't know, I don't know. By the time I thought of it, it was too late. And how was I supposed to know that the Mob would go after me?"

"Oh, right, Ken, you never have anything to do with anything, it all just happens to you."

He let his head roll back on his shoulders and stared at the ceiling. He sighed, and said, "All right, it's my fault and I'm sorry. But I've got it worked out so that you and the kids will be safe. But you're going to have to do some things, precautions that you're not going to like altogether. It's the only way, just hear me out."

He reached into his back pocket and pulled out the manila envelope and placed it on the kitchen table.

"What's that?" she said.

"Back child support. Now, here's what it is."

Grace pulled back warily but listened.

The night passed as he laid it out. They talked into the early hours of the morning, splitting a few Yuenglings along the way.

Grace looked tired now, half-resting on the tabletop. "I've got to get up, soon," she said, half asleep.

"Grace, you haven't even gone to bed yet."

She smiled, the first time in years, he imagined, at least when he'd been around. Then, she frowned, "Ken, do you think . . . do you ever think that if we had stayed together that somehow all of this wouldn't have happened, couldn't have happened?"

Genuine sorrow swept over him then, the real deep thing he'd felt before when he was alone and knew why he was alone no matter what Grace had done.

"Hell, Grace, how could we have ever stayed together?"

Ken stood up, kissed her on the top of her head, and slipped out the back door.

He padded silently to the shed in the backyard and was annoyed to find a padlock on the door. The asshole, he thought. He pulled his belt from his trousers and wedged it through the loop of the lock. A quick yank and it was sprung.

Everything in the shed had been reorganized, another moment of concern, until he found his box still hidden up in the rafters in the back. He grabbed the sweatshirt, some tape, vinyl gloves, a few small tools, and left.

Ken managed to make it back to Bea's room just as light began to consume the lower edges of the night's darkness. Bea stirred and stretched. Ken sat on the edge of the bed next to her.

"Joe was here looking for you. I put him off, but I think he's getting suspicious."

She sat up next to him, hunched over. She wore a cotton undershirt with spaghetti straps and a bikini brief. "I guess our torrid love affair is about over," she said.

"That's all right," Ken said, "so's the trial. I will miss the torrid part, though."

Late in the morning, Ken and the other jurors sat, looking as bored as they felt. Harry Lupino asked another witness one question after another about Mob minutiae. The witness, a very nervous fellow in his mid-thirties, wearing an ill-fitting suit, answered questions about delivering bags to Innunzio's social club without ever knowing what was inside. More circumstantial evidence thought Ken.

"Your honor, that concludes the questions I have for this witness."

Ken jumped. Had he fallen asleep?

"All right, thank you, Mr. Lupino. Cross examine, Mr. McCarthy?"

"No, your honor, no questions for this witness."

"Okay, then let's have lunch," said the judge.

"All rise," said the bailiff, mostly to the backs of the people already leaving the courtroom.

Outside of the jurors' room, Joe the guard stopped Ken in the hallway waiting for the elevator.

"Uh, Ken, I need to see you for a sec."

Mildly surprised, Ken said, "Sure Joe, what's up?"

Joe lowered his voice, "The, uh, the P.A., he wants to see you. Lupino. The prosecutor."

"He does? What for?"

"I dunno," the guard said, "but it isn't ordinary."

"Huh."

"Yeah," Joe said. "I'll take you to him. He's in a meeting room on the tenth floor."

They rode the elevator down several floors, and Joe led Ken to a meeting room. Harry Lupino sat in a wooden chair on the far side of a conference table. Ken saw another suit sitting next to him on the right. Round-faced with a heavy beard and a blocky build, the new guy sported a close-shaved perimeter of hair that crowned his otherwise balding head. To distract, he wore a lavish moustache. In his dull, rumpled gray suit, he represented the exact opposite of the slick, sharp-dressed Lupino.

"Please sit down," Lupino said, gesturing to a straight-back wooden chair opposite him. Ken walked over to sit.

"All right, Mr. Pruitt. This is Mr. Perry Sanchez, another federal attorney. I've asked him here to conduct this interview to ensure that no violations occur."

Sanchez nodded his head at Ken without saying a word.

Lupino continued, "That means that we won't be discussing the case, Mr. Pruitt, not any part of it. That would be illegal and grounds for a mistrial. A mistrial would mean that the four years put into this case by the FBI, the DEA, and every other federal agency and officer involved in investigating organized crime, including myself, would be wasted. The four months you and the other jurors have spent sitting in the courtroom, all wasted, gone up in smoke." Lupino pointed his finger at the ceiling, "Poof. Do you understand what I'm saying, Mr. Pruitt? I can't let that happen, and I'm sure that you don't want it to happen either. Am I right?"

Ken shrugged and nodded his head.

"Okay, then, we will not be talking about the case. In fact, I won't be talking about the case. In fact, I won't be talking at all except when circumstances require me to, you understand? Mr. Sanchez will be conducting this interview."

Lupino paused, then nodded at Sanchez.

"Mr. Pruitt, it has come to our attention that an attempt has been made, at least one, to tamper with the jury." Sanchez waited, staring at Ken.

Sitting calmly, Ken crossed his legs.

"You know what that means?" Sanchez continued. "Exactly what Mr. Lupino just stated. This entire case, the time you've spent here and everyone else's could come to nothing. That's millions of dollars at risk, Mr. Pruitt. It's very unusual in this day and age to sequester a jury because of the expense. That's how important Mr. Lupino and his superiors value this prosecution."

"Worst of all, that shitbird piece of shit Pete Innunzio could walk," Lupino spit.

"Harry," Sanchez said.

"Yeah, Perry, I know. Mr. Pruitt, please pay no attention to what I just said about that cocksucker Innunzio."

"Harry!"

"Okay, okay. No more about Innunzio, I promise."

"You see, Mr. Pruitt, this could be a very serious problem. So, I'm going to ask you a series of questions and I want the truth. You understand, Mr. Pruitt, we need to know the truth."

Ken nodded his head again.

"Now," said Sanchez, "do you know about anyone on the jury being approached?"

"No," said Ken without hesitation.

"Anyone at all, by phone or a note? A visitor, perhaps?"

"No."

Sanchez paused. "You're sure you understand the repercussions? You're absolutely sure?"

"Jesus, yes, okay? What, do you think I need a lawyer here? I have one, a divorce lawyer, but that's all I can afford right now. I can barely afford her, to tell you the truth."

Sternly, Sanchez said, "You will not need representation. No, sir. Absolutely not." He allowed a beat to pass. "So, no one you know of on the jury was approached, acted ill at ease, anything like that."

"Nope, none. I'd be the first to tell you if it was me. No one's heard anything."

Harry Lupino sat back in his chair.

"That's very interesting, Mr. Pruitt," said Sanchez, "because we know of one juror who was approached. On a prepaid cell phone left in a brown bag lunch in the courthouse lobby. This witness was threatened, then offered a bribe." Sanchez paused again. "This doesn't sound at all familiar to you?"

"No. Not at all," said Ken.

"That is surprising. It's surprising because members of organized crime usually look for insurance. They try to cover all of their bets. Why compromise one juror when they might be able to turn another? Sounds pretty smart, don't you think?"

Ken shrugged, "I wouldn't know."

"Hmm. Very surprising, because of course, you see, once Mr. Lupino heard about this, he had to check it out. But he had to be circumspect as well. He could not risk talking to jury members for the reasons he stated earlier. So, he followed a different strategy first. He started by reviewing the courthouse security DVDs dating to the beginning of the trial."

Ken tensed minutely.

"Do you know what he saw almost immediately? He watched you walk into the lobby on one of the very first trial days and pick up a brown bag left on a bench. Surprising, huh?"

"I guess so," Ken said.

Lupino leaned forward. "What was in the bag, Pruitt?"

"Lunch."

Lupino glanced at Sanchez. "Lunch. Just lunch?"

"Yeah," said Ken.

"No cell phone," Lupino said.

"No. Just a sandwich, a piece of fruit, a Coke, and a chocolate chip cookie, one of those large kind."

"The soft kind, right?"

Ken shrugged, "It was stale."

Lupino scowled. "So, . . . just lunch."

"Yes."

Sanchez said, "Your statement is that you went down to the lobby to pick up a bag left on a bench for you, and the only thing in it was lunch."

Ken nodded.

"You fucking idiot," snapped Lupino, "you expect us to believe this? What do you think, we're fucking stupid?"

"Harry," Sanchez said, grasping Lupino's arm. Lupino sat back, burning. Ken sat placidly, silent.

"The problem is, Mr. Pruitt," Sanchez said, "we watched more of the security videos and saw other jurors picking up brown bags left on the same bench. We have them on tape, too. What about them? Those bags didn't have cell phones in them either? The other jurors weren't threatened and offered bribes?"

"Maybe they were. I don't know, you'll have to ask them."

"But you were not."

"No," Ken replied.

"There was no cell phone in your lunch bag."

"No."

"Jesus Christ, you—" Lupino muttered. Sanchez gestured and Lupino sat back again.

"All right, no cell phone. Then," Sanchez continued, "let me ask you this, Mr. Pruitt. How did you know the brown bag was out there for you on the bench?

Ken hesitated. "I ordered it. From a favorite sandwich shop of mine. I thought it might be the last good hoagie I'd get for a while."

"Really?" Lupino said. "Let me guess the name of the shop. Mickey's Deli Sandwiches. Is that it?"

Ken shifted slightly in his seat.

Lupino pressed, "You see, that was the name on the bag picked up by the other juror. Is that where you ordered your sandwiches? "

Pausing again before answering, Ken said "Sure. On Baron Street. I'm a carpenter, I had a job near there one time. I found out they have good sandwiches."

"Mickey's is a known haunt of Innunzio's people. Are you aware of that, Mr. Pruitt?"

"I know it's a Mob joint," Ken answered, "everyone does. I don't know if Innunzio has anything to do with it. The food's good."

Lupino said, "You expect us to believe that you had a bag lunch sent to you from Mickey's, a notorious Scarfo front, and you didn't find a cell phone inside?"

"I ordered the sandwich and there was no phone in the bag. Believe me, if there was I would have reported it."

"And the other jurors?" Sanchez asked.

"I ordered sandwiches for a couple of them sort of as a joke. You know, the condemned's last meal before nothing but a steady died of bad hotel food. After a while, everyone was ordering them. You should try one, they're good."

Sanchez said back. Then, he said, "Mr. Pruitt, you are sure about this? There are consequences for obstructing justice and accepting a bribe."

"I swear, I don't know about any phone or any bribe, just some sandwiches. Maybe the guy you let go ordered one, stuck a phone in the bag, and came to you with a story. I don't know."

"How did you know the juror we dismissed was a man?" Sanchez said.

Ken frowned, looking exasperated. "Guy, gal, whatever. Whoever you let go, okay?"

Lupino joined in, calmer now. "Look, Pruitt," "you're seeing this all wrong. This is your ticket out of here. Just tell us what happened, and we'll have to dismiss you from the jury to preclude even the perception of any impropriety."

"This is the first I've heard of this, believe me. If I knew anything, I'd tell you. I'd love to get out of here."

Sanchez and Lupino exchanged glances.

"All right, Mr. Pruitt," said Sanchez. "You can go for now. You should know, however, that we will be interviewing the other jurors and if their accounts do not match yours, you will be held for obstruction of justice. Do you understand?"

Ken nodded his head.

"Very well. Officer Fagley will escort you back to the juror's room.

Ken stood up and left the room with Joe.

Sanchez looked at Lupino, who said, "Well? Can you believe this bullshit about a brown bag and no phone?"

"I don't know what to believe. Maybe he's telling the truth, but we better talk to the rest of them. How many other jurors picked up bags?"

"Just two," Lupino said, "aside from the kid that blew the whistle. Maybe Pruitt's telling the truth. Maybe he just bought the kid a sandwich and the little shit cooked the whole cell thing up to get off the jury."

"Then it worked, didn't it?" said Sanchez

Lupino stiffened, "He was excused for medical reasons."

"Unhuh. Jesus." He gazed up at the ceiling, then said, "All right, let's talk to the other two. But, if the kid was telling the truth, who knows how many others were contacted? We can't dismiss them all, we only have so many alternates. The judge will declare a mistrial if we lose more than two or three."

"If any of this gets out he might do that anyway. So, what the fuck can we do?" Lupino asked.

"I think you better get your star witness in here as fast as possible and hope that their plan was for a mistrial, not an outright acquittal."

Lupino whined, "Jesus Christ, what a mess."

"Also," said Sanchez, "have someone keep an eye on Pruitt. Something about that guy makes me wonder."

Ken walked into the jurors' room and looked around. They all seemed to be there except one. Bea and Ira are sitting at the far end of the table. Ken strolled over and said in a low voice, "Have you seen Colin?"

Ira said, "He's gone, excused from the jury. They didn't say why."

"Fuck," Ken breathed. He lowered his voice more and told them,

"Colin got a bag with a phone. He told the prosecutor."

"He did?" Bea said. She look hopeful, "Then, maybe it's about to end. They'll call it a mistrial, right?"

Ken flashed her a quick look of alarm.

"No. I just met with Lupino and another fed. They got me on a security camera picking up the bag. I was the first, but they say they saw others. I swore that I didn't get a phone and they sort of believed me, even though it's ludicrous. They want to believe me. They got four years invested in this trial and they don't want to start over. Which means they'll believe you, too, if you say the same thing. Tell them I ordered the sandwiches for you as a joke, but don't tell them about the phones, nothing."

"Why can't we just do what Colin did and get thrown off the jury?" Bea asked plaintively.

Ken shook his head, "No good. They're pissed about this, they threatened to charge me with obstruction because I didn't report it to them. They'll do the same to you, too."

"Shit," Ira spat. "No wonder he looked guilty when he slunk outta here."

"Colin didn't know anything," Ken said, "he just saw his chance is all."

"They can't really do that," Bea said, "can they? Arrest us?"

"I don't know, but we better hope that they wrap this trial up soon. Anyway, you look at it, it's not good for us for it to keep going like this."

"So, what do we do in the meantime?" Ira said.

"Act like you don't know anything. I dumped the phones, so they can't do anything to you if you just sit tight. Maybe Colin's done us all a favor, maybe they'll kick it into high gear rather than be stuck with a mistrial, start pointing fingers at us."

Bea sighed, looking down, deeply worried. Ken gritted his teeth.

"Colin, that fucking little shit," barked Ira.

Everyone had taken their seat when McCarthy ushered Pistol Pete to the defendant's table. Now, they sat and waited for the judge to enter and make them all stand up again. After three tough days, Ken felt at ease. Grace had called him on his cell, said "Done," then hung up. He'd slept well for the following two nights. He could wait forever, now, at rest. He crossed his legs, in sneakers and jeans of course, but also wearing his old sports coat again, over a dark blue sweatshirt. Bea glanced his way, and he gave her a big smile.

The judge entered, making them all stand up again. He turned to the prosecutor and said, "Mr. Lupino, are you ready to proceed?"

"I am, your honor. I would like to call to the stand my last witness, who is being escorted here from the FDC right now. He should arrive within the next 15 minutes."

So, now, thought Ken. The gallery seemed to inhale as one, letting out a collective rush of air that changed into murmurs. The Judge raised his voice slightly, "Order. Okay, Counselor, we'll take a 15-minute recess." He smacked his gavel down once, then rose and walked back to his chambers. Everyone else stood up at once and milled about, unsure about what to do, whether to go out into the hallway for such a short break.

Ken strode to the door leading from court to the jury's room inside to the private restroom. After locking the stall door, he took his jacket off and hung it from the hook on the back. Rooting through its pockets, he dug out the vinyl gloves and stuffed them into his back pants pocket. Then he quietly cracked open the door. Seeing no one, he walked briskly out the door opposite the courtroom into the hall. He turned away from the elevators and headed to the emergency stairway. Quickly, he pulled open the door usually secured shut except when someone taped the lock mechanism open. He'd done just that on his last training run, thank you Joe, he mouthed silently. Also, thanks to the old Watergate burglars who showed how not to do it.

Ken dashed down the stairs, faster than running up but trickier, too. Reaching the basement, he ran down the hall to the engineering maintenance closet, locked, which he forced in no time. He flicked on the light, found what he was looking for, a long, thin, metal rod with a simple perpendicular key shape on the end. He gingerly shoved the rod inside his belt, then sped toward the loading dock. Outside the side entrance just around the corner where the jury took breaks, he unrolled the hood from inside of his sweatshirt. He put on his dark blue vinyl gloves, then pulled the hood over his head while peering through the door's narrow window with chicken wire embedded in the glass. No one.

Ken reached in his pocket for one of the two lunch cells he still had. He tapped in the number and waited.

"James A. Byrne Federal Courthouse, how can I direct your call?"

"There is a bomb on the 16th floor ready to go off."

He snapped the cell in half, flung it toward the dumpsters, and bolted back inside. He raced the length of the hall and around the corner to the elevator that led up to the courtroom holding areas. Out of his jean's change pocket he yanked a hard, plastic key he'd made in his hotel room and inserted it into the elevator slot. He heard the generator come to life at the same time as the sirens outside. He ducked to one side and waited forever.

The elevator stopped; the doors opened. Ken wrapped one arm around the doorway to hold the door fast and dipped his head in quickly. Empty.

He jumped in, inserted the plastic key and pushed the 16th floor button. The elevator began to rise as fire alarms sounded throughout the building. While the elevator rose, Ken tied the hood drawstring tight to his face so that only his eyes could be seen. He pulled the rod from his pants and held it out in front of him.

The elevator reached the 16th floor and the doors opened. He could hear alarms yammering throughout the building, including one that filled the hallway with noise. Ken pushed the red button in the elevator, so the doors stayed open. He tucked himself in the front corner, out of sight, and waited.

He could hear voices in the hall, indiscernible because of the alarms. Ken waited until he heard them at the elevator doorway.

"I don't know," one voice said, "a prank, maybe."

Ken moved out to find Earl McCarthy and Pete Innunzio standing at the door flanked by two courthouse guards. He grabbed Innunzio by the collar, twisted him around and yanked him back with the metal rod pressed across his throat. McCarthy and the two guards stood stunned, completely surprised.

The guards made moves toward their guns. Ken shook his head, "I'll crush his windpipe."

One guard dropped his hand to his side, but the other still fumbled with his holster: Joe Fagley.

Shit. Shifting to hold Innunzio with one forearm, Ken stepped out and snapped the rod out like a rapier across Joe's hand, which jerked straight up. "Ow!" he cried, dropping his gun.

Innunzio started hacking from the tightness of his grip as Ken muscled him into the elevator and turned the key. The doors slowly closed. He pushed the button for the 19th floor and released Innunzio, who fell to the floor, still coughing, his glasses halfway up his brow.

Slowly, he regained his breath. Deliberately, he adjusted his glasses and raised his eyes to Ken. "Who the hell are you?"

Ken said, "You don't recognize me, Pete?" Ken loosened the drawstring and pulled back his hood. Innunzio squinted, then said, "You look familiar. You're on the jury. You're that guy, the Seal."

Ken nodded, "Yes I am. I work for you, Pete."

The doors opened and Ken grabbed Innunzio by the back of his suit collar. He pulled him upright and marched him outside, taking the plastic key with him as he stepped out, but first pushing the button for the 20th floor.

"What are you doing?" Innunzio shouted above the ringing alarms. "You've been paid, what's this all about?"

Ken watched the doors close and listened for the hum of the elevator rising. Then, he inserted the keyed end of the metal rod into a small hole in the outer door of the elevator. He twisted it until the doors opened.

Innunzio struggled, crying out, "You better stop or you're gonna get hurt! What are you doing? What the fuck do you want?"

Ken pulled him close to his face, "You ought to know, Pete, you're a family man," and tossed him down the shaft.

He heard the screaming, which was soon lost to the pounding of the alarms. No thud, either. Too bad.

Ken removed the rod and dropped it down the elevator shaft as the doors closed. He ran to the stairwell at the opposite end of the floor and opened the door, pulling the tape loose from the door and sticking it in his jeans. He ran down the stairs to the 16th floor, tucking his hood inside his sweatshirt and the gloves in his pocketsts. Scanning the hall outside, he saw that they'd all been evacuated. He quickly sped through the hall to the men's room, where he turned the gloves inside out to wash them thoroughly. He broke up the key, then flushed it, the gloves, and the balled-up tape down the toilet, one by one, making sure that they all cleared. He put on his jacket and trotted to the stairways again.

Across the mall, Bea, stamping her feet from the cold, was the first one to see him. "My God, Ken, where've you been? Didn't you hear the alarm?"

"Yeah, but I was in the bathroom. Sometimes you can't leave no matter what's going on."

"There's been a bomb threat," she said, "and Joe told us that someone kidnapped Innunzio! They don't know where he is!"

"You're kidding," Ken said. "What do you think that means?"

"I don't know," she said, "but maybe they'll let us go home."

Ken nodded his head, "I think they might."

The other lunch cell rang. Ken smiled, ignoring it. He reached into his jacket and pulled out an envelope. "Here, Bea. This is for you."

"What is it?"

"Just some numbers and how to use them. It's a going away present, for torridness rendered."

She smiled sheepishly, "Oh. Mustn't be much, then."

"Well. You might be surprised," Ken said.

He turned to Ira and said, "This one's for you, Ira."

The cell kept ringing.

"You going to answer that?" Ira asked.

"Yeah, I guess," Ken said. Still smiling, he moved away.

"What the hell happened?"

"You tell me, Lou. Lupino was about to produce the star witness when everything blew up. Abbruzzese never even made it into the building, they hustled his ass right out of here before I ever had a chance. And now, Innunzio's missing."

"I know that, shithead, why do you think I'm calling?"

"I don't know, Louie, this entire detail has been completely fucked. I was ready to go, then all this."

"You don't know where he is?"

"Hell, no. They evacuated us out of the building, I just heard he was gone. Did you get him out?"

"Don't be stupid, what good would that do?"

"Who's stupid? You could've come for him as insurance, if you didn't think I really could take care of Abbruzzese. Or maybe you have other problems at your end, Louie, maybe someone doesn't want your boss back home and tipped off Solito. Like you, maybe. In the meantime, here I am, stuck."

"Don't make up fairy tales. You got our money, pal."

"Yeah, and I was ready to do my part. Now what?"

"You give back the money for starters."

"Can't do that, Lou, it's gone. I gave it to my wife."

"Your wife? Your ex-wife. I got news for you, sport. She's gone."

Ken smiled silently, then said coldly, "What do you mean? Where is she, what did you do to her?"

"Don't get your ass up, we didn't do nothing. Just checking up on her and she's gone, left town. Clothes gone, bathroom products, all that kind of stuff."

"What about my kids?"

"Shit, I don't know, gone with her. All we found was some asshole nosing about the house, asking about her himself."

"Asshole, huh?" Again, Ken smiled.

"Never mind that, she's gone and with your money, or so you say. Any way you look at it, you're dead, Kenny boy, Navy hard-ass or whatever, you're still done."

"Sure I am, Lou," Ken said. "Or, I could make good on the money."

Silence. Like in their first calls, Ken thought, until Lou said, "How you going to do that?"

"Solito. He's got to be of equal or more value than ten Jerry Abbruzzeses. I'll take care of Solito to square us on the money."

Again, Lou didn't respond right away.

"How you going to do that?"

"I'm a Navy hard-ass, remember? Nobody will see me coming, they won't expect me. I can get to anyone, Lou, even you if you still think you have to get to me. Better we pool our resources to take care of our problems together rather than risk each other's well-being."

After another long pause, Lou sighed, then said in a small voice, "I'll have to check with Mr. Innunzio first."

"Okay, Lou. Run it past him when he turns up. Remember, I work for you."

He smiled, closed the cell phone, and walked back to the others waiting on the mall.

Cleaning House

"I don't understand," said Marcia the Caterer, "Why?"

"I have a better offer," Sheila said.

"What do you mean? Are they giving you more money? If it's more money, I'm sure that we can work it out. Do you feel that you've been mistreated?"

"Of course not."

"Then, it's more money."

"No, that's not it."

"Then what is it?" Marcia said, with something like desperation peeking out from behind her usually steady eyes.

It's your J.C. Penney's furniture, Sheila said silently, your off-the-rack designer dresses and suits that look so good on you, though God knows how you keep your figure with all the food around, and your tastefully framed reprints of Modigliani, Monet, Pollack, and DeKoonig, your Hecht's china and Revere silverware.

"It's logistics," she said. "It's just easier to get to."

Poor Marcia wilted. Sheila referred Juana to her, as she always did with castoffs. Usually in a few weeks the nice ones would call her and leave a message on her machine thanking her, saying how they loved Juana. But of course, that first moment when she announced that she was leaving killed them.

"I don't know what I'm going to do," Marcia sputtered, nearly in tears, "No one has ever done the silver like you, no one has ever really cleaned the oven fan before."

Yeah, Sheila sighed, Marcia would call in her thanks. And she had no idea of how thankful she should be.

Sheila walked into the Arlington World Value Pawn Shop and looked over the watches while she waited. The man in front of the counter turned to leave, folding fresh, green bills into his wallet as he went out the door.

"Sheila Hurley, how are you?"

"Okay, Leo," she replied, ducking under the bellies of a dozen guitars hanging from the ceiling as she stepped over to the heavy-set man behind the counter. In his late forties and about an inch shorter than herself, his skin seemed tan year-round, though she knew for a fact that he hardly ever left town. "How are you?" she said, "How's your wife?"

"Happy and fat."

"Oh? Does that mean you won't be hitting on me today?"

He gave her a wounded look, "Sheila, it's my job."

She smiled wryly.

"So, what can I do for you? I haven't seen you in years it seems, months."

"Yeah, well, you know. I've been working."

"Sure. How's school going?"

"It's going. Doing independent study. You know, reading for the exam."

"Unhuh. That's what you said the last time, right? Three months ago."

"Hey, comps are tough. They cover Old English, Beowulf, all the way up to contemporary lit. Then there's my thesis."

"Yeah, but Sheila, you been working on this thing for as long as I know you," he rolled his eyes almost up to his wiry gray hair, thinking back, "It must be a couple of years."

"Leo, give me a break. It's not everyone who can cram an eighteen-month program into three years."

"Yeah, yeah," he said, "three years and counting." He closed the cash register. "So, how else are you? Still seeing that guy, the uh, the history guy?"

"Cultural anthropology. No, he's gone."

"Oh, I'm sorry to hear that. What happened?"

"I aired him out," she said with a toss of her head that made her long falling blond hair flip like a horsetail. "He turned out to be politically incorrect. He decided to go to law school."

"No shit? Gonna become one of those, is he?"

"Looks that way."

Leo shook his head, parting his lips just a little to allow a small smile to show, including the tiny gap between his very white teeth. "And you're still the avid commie, right?"

"You bet, Leo, I'm not changing. Socialism will rise again."

"Sure. In the meantime, you're still cleaning their houses."

"I have to pay the rent, I have to pay tuition. And, I have my plans."

"Yeah, so you've told me, Thailand, the clinic. Is that why you're here after so long?" She lifted her hand in a conciliatory gesture, "Well, to see you. You know, to keep in touch. Really, things are starting to come together. Depending upon certain schedules, we could be talking about early spring. I'm going over now for a run-through on a new house that could fill out the week."

"I thought you already had a full schedule."

"Nope. Gave one up. The caterer."

"Didn't meet your standards, huh?"

"That's accurate."

"Unhuh. Well, when you get it all into place, Sheila, give me a shout. I'm always here."

Her voice became almost solemn. "I'm serious, Leo. I'm going to be dropping by a lot more often, now, to arrange things. You'll be ready?"

This time his grin spread wide across his face. "Sheila, I'm always ready."

As she zipped down the Lee Highway toward the bridge, she

thought of how it pissed her off when people ragged her about school, as though it was like a summer at the beach. Let them try to hold down a job, a physically exhausting job, five days a week, then hit the books every night. So, what if it was taking her longer than the average daytime student, it was the same with law and business students in night school. Man, she thought, when Leo started in on that stuff, it was like he was saying that she was a scatterbrain. Christ, if he didn't think she was organized, he should talk to her clients, let him talk to Marcia, for God's sake.

Okay, she thought with a grimace, she hadn't been doing much reading lately or any work on her thesis. But the degree really didn't matter anymore, though she did want to finish it.

She grabbed the page of directions next to her, glanced at them, then flicked the sheet away. She downshifted to make the turn onto MacArthur Boulevard, wrinkling her nose at the same time as she picked up the smell of seeping gasoline, a constant reminder to get the car fixed.

On the edge of Bethesda, the development was called Riverrun, a single word to distinguish it from several others with the same name but spelled with two words. As she drove through, she recognized the setting, a bunch of big, new, million-dollar houses stuffed on half-acre parcels, each surrounded by a few young trees. The new client worked for American Fidelity S & L, a vice president, a good candidate, she thought. She wondered if he operated like a cowboy or assumed a conservative pose as he wheeled and dealed.

She reached the house and slowly pulled into a wide driveway in front of a three-car garage. The house was a scaled-down version of a Hyannis Port model, finished in gray siding, with dormers and skylights on different levels. She parked next to a red BMW and sighed to herself. Well, at least it wasn't a Porsche.

"Hey!" a voice called out, "an old Beetle. Where'd you get that?"

Startled, Sheila looked out her side window and saw him sitting in his car. He got out, walked over, and leaned in on her sill.

"What year is it?" he said, looking past her at the dashboard, then in the back.

She found herself staring at him, at his wavy hair carefully slicked back, at his thin, black wire-rim glasses that did nothing to hide his blue eyes. His lean, slender build finished him off perfectly for an ad in *GQ*.

Oh, brother, she said to herself.

"I used to have one of these in school. What year?"

"I don't know," she said, "Seventy-four, I think. It belonged to my folks."

"Unhuh." He finally remembered to look at her. "You must be Sheila Hurley. I'm Mark Roth."

"Hello."

"Come on in. I was just getting a map from my car. Planning a trip to Hilton Head in April. Going to drive my Beemer."

Beemer. Good God.

"Yeah, I know, the yuppie cliché, but what the hell. A couple of years ago I was trying to get onto 395 one afternoon to make a meeting for which I was already late," he said as he led her up the walk, "and I got stuck behind this BMW. Well, after missing three lights in a row, I was ready to stand on my horn to make the guy look back so I could yell at him, 'C'mon, buddy, you got the ultimate-fucking-driving machine, so fucking drive!'"

Her eyes snapped up from the slate sidewalk in surprise. He looked back at her with a crooked grin, "But I didn't do it. Instead, right then and there I decided to get one, to show them all how to fucking drive."

They went through one of the double doors into the vestibule. Her eyes automatically inventoried the tile floor and the mahogany side table with the gilded gold mirror above it next to the stairway. She made mental notes of special cleaning agents she might need as he brought her into the living room, a huge space with large French doors at either end, the rear ones opening out on a patio next to a sizeable pool. He motioned toward one of two white couches set on a white, thick pile rug around a white brick fireplace. He said, "Sit down and we'll talk. Can I get you something to drink?"

"Excuse me, Mr. Roth, but if we're going to begin discussing specific tasks, it's really better for your wife to be here, too."

"Not married no more," he said with his hands palm out in defense. "I live alone. No dogs, no cats, no attachments. So, if you want to run away with me to some tropical paradise, I'm ready."

A strange wind rustled through her, and he said, "Hey, just kidding. Let's go, I'll show you around."

He took her upstairs, and she noted the Henredon bed set and the tall Sherrill dresser made of cherry wood. Juana would not be getting this guy, she thought.

"Is this a great place, or what?" he said. "I just moved in last month. I really love it."

I'll bet, she thought. "You have a beautifully appointed home, Mr. Roth."

"You think so? Here," he said, "take a look at these."

From a pile next to the bed he grabbed a bunch of dress shirts and held them out, some white, some pale blue, others striped, the rest a variety of pastels. She looked at them, wrinkled and obviously dirty, then at him with a puzzled expression.

"What do you think?" he said.

"What? Do you want me to send them to the cleaners?"

"No, look," he said, stroking the top one, "Feel. The best Sea Island cotton, from the Custom Shop."

She stared at him. After a pause, she said flatly, "I have never seen such beautiful shirts."

He drew back, then laughed ruefully, "But you're not impressed, Daisy."

He tossed the shirts in a pile at the end of the bed.

She took a step forward and said, "Mr. Roth, I'm sorry if I offended you," and, surprising herself, she meant it. The guy was stereotypical, but he seemed embarrassed that she'd seen through him so fast.

"No, no, I'm not insulted. You found me out, and I'm red-faced."

"Mr. Roth, really—"

"Don't worry about it, Sheila—Ms. Hurley. Just don't get the wrong impression, okay? I was just messing around."

She didn't say anything, couldn't think of anything to say.

"I suppose you think I'm a real asshole showing off to the new cleaning lady—person."

"No," she said solemnly "not at all."

"Sure. You think we all work at the Alzheimer's S and L. You know, the bank where people deposit early and forget about it later?"

She laughed, suddenly cutting it short. She stood locked in place, feeling her head ballooning as she took in the horrific words. She had laughed. And he had known she would, as though somehow, he recognized her as the type.

"Close your mouth, Sheila, it isn't that way. American Fidelity is a good outfit." He flashed a smile, an exposure of white teeth that tightened glorious olive skin over cutting cheekbones, carving impossibly deep hollows beneath them.

"And you're not the ordinary cleaning lady, either, using Fitzgerald to dump on me. Interesting."

"Mr. Roth, I am truly sorry about this, this unfortunate beginning."

"Yeah, you really blew it."

She had, she thought. And she didn't want to lose this guy. It would set her back another three months, maybe a year, she told herself. Look at his polo shirt, Sans Tambours N. Trompettes for God's sake.

"But I tell you what," he said. "You can make it up to me. I'll let you keep the job, if—"

Her stomach sank. The guy had no imagination after all; the job was gone.

"—you go to dinner with me tomorrow night."

Hope leaped within her, then quieted. This wasn't workable either. She couldn't do this anymore than the obvious if she was to clean his house. Not to mention, she thought, that in spite of what he said, socio-politically speaking, he still was as reprehensible as they came.

"Yeah, I know. If you work for me, we shouldn't go out," he said, "But my mom used to clean my room and I take her out to dinner on every one of her birthdays whether she wants to or not. Come on, what do you have to lose at this point?"

Nothing or everything, she figured.

"Come on. The worst you'll get is a great dinner. Come on?" He smiled, "No go, huh? Okay, let's see the rest of the house. So, you're a student, right?"

"You should of taken him up on it, Sheila. Why not?"

"You're out of your mind, Leo. He's the goddamn Antichrist, for Christ's sake."

"Come on, he can't be that bad, you said he treated you okay even after you roughed him up. He's good looking, too, right?"

"Very. But I'm not going to let hormones dictate my life. The man's wicked."

"Naw, Sheila, I saw it in the paper. American Fidelity even helped build some shelters for the homeless."

"And who made them homeless by foreclosing on their mortgages, for crying out loud?"

"Sheila, you don't know that."

"Well, somebody kicked them out. Leo, this guy is not for me."

"Yeah, yeah, I hear you. But I think you may be passing up on a good thing, you know?"

"Oh, I'm not passing up on anything. Leo, you don't think I'm serious about any of this, do you?"

"No, no, I take you serious. So, tell me what's new?"

"Okay. It's really shaping up."

Fred Negri wore his gray hair in a fabulously permed bouffant. His thick glasses also served as a style statement, like Lefty Lazar's rather than evidence of his terrible eyesight. He and his wife had built a Palm Beach ranch in Potomac with a swimming pool between the garage and the living room, screened front and back. Sheila didn't particularly like the stark style of the house with its tiled hallways and Spartan gray carpeting. But it was the easiest house for her to clean, and they did own a Frank Lloyd Wright dining room set, a Roche-Bobois tango bed, and some Knoll pieces.

After the first meeting, Sheila had never seen Fred's wife again, but proof of her existence lay in every closet—shoes by Robert Clergerie, Charles Jourdan, Bottega Veneta, Mancini, Gucci, and Stuart Weitz; clothes by Missoni, Gianni Versace, Donna Karan, Claude Montana, Joseph Albond; cocktail gowns by Oleg Cassini and Chanel, accessories by Mandfredi and Boris leBeau. Put most kindly, Mrs. Negri's taste was eclectic; put plainly, she didn't care how it looked on the outside, only what name was stitched on the inside. Even the label on her perfume read Custom-designed for Ms. Rita Negri by Mamounas.

And, of course, she had furs—Sorbara, Calvin Klein, Saks, Jandel, and a riot of others. Fred would pull one out of a closet, saying, "Here, try this on," as he threw it around Sheila's shoulders. "Blue fox, the latest, just in."

"Very nice, Mr. Negri."

"I'll get you one. Because you're so good to us. Below wholesale."

"I couldn't, Mr. Negri."

"Can't afford it? It's yours. An early Christmas present. You're a terrific girl, Sheila."

"So, is he putting the moves on you, too?" asked Leo.

"No, he just loves to do that stuff. He told me he gave one to the cook, too."

"But you didn't take the pelt, naturally."

"Of course not. I told him I was allergic."

"Ah! Still, you could have sold it."

"Sure. Anyway, I'm lucky to keep them. They're way rich enough to afford live-in help, but Fred likes me. They're easy, too. They ride the car train to Miami every year and stay for two months. They have a house on Williams Island. This year they're leaving February 15th."

"Yeah?"

"And the Dolans are going back to Illinois to visit his in-laws for Easter. They leave on the 29th of March."

"They're your Tuesdays?"

"They're Wednesday," Sheila said. "The Negris are Tuesday, the Rosens Thursday."

"Rosen's the doctor, right?"

"A physician. They go to Chicago every year at Passover, since both his parents and hers live there. They stay through the week."

"Okay," Leo said.

"This year Passover starts on the 29th. Easter is the 31st."

"I'm following you. The Dolans, the Rosens, and the Negris all will be gone by the 29th."

"Exactly. That leaves American Fidelity and the Merritts. Mr. S and L has already talked about a trip in his bright, shiny red BMW to Hilton Head in April. The Merritts usually go to the antique show in New York for two days, though they haven't told me yet whether or not they're going. But if I get lucky . . ." she said.

She nodded her head and left.

On Friday morning, she drove slowly into his driveway, tentatively peering out of her windshield for his car. No red Beemer. She parked and began to transport her materials into the house storage area. Then, she moved upstairs to begin on the ceilings and the walls. She dry-mopped the ceilings and wiped down the walls, wiped the picture frames, then dusted and polished the furniture, leaving the vacuuming for last. She cleaned the bathroom, then went downstairs for lunch, after which she would do the first floor.

Her reverie was broken by the muted drum of a car engine downshifting as it approached the house. She looked at her watch and was surprised to find that it was four-thirty. After storing the cleaning materials, she walked out to her car. She half waved to Mark Roth who just then was getting out of his car. He walked over to her, smiling.

"Hi," he said. He carried his jacket draped over his briefcase, and his tie was pulled down from his collar.

"I heard you drive in a while ago," she said, smiling herself. "Was your seatbelt stuck?"

"No," he said with a slight laugh, "I was listening to NPR. Fun stuff, you know?"

"Sure," she said. After an awkward pause, she said, "Well, I guess I'll move along."

"Okay. Have a nice evening."

She started to go, then did a half-turn back. "You know, I read that American Fidelity has done some good work for the homeless."

"Huh? Oh, yeah," he said, "do we have a great PR guy or what?"

She laughed, "Sure. Anyway, I still feel really bad about last week."

"Yeah. I know," he said, "and I'm still hurt."

"Oh," she said.

"You bet. You treat me like shit and you won't even go out with me? Listen, I don't know if you've noticed, but I am drop-dead good-looking." He struck a sideways pose, his hands on his waist, his nose in the air, his teeth flashing.

She couldn't control a burst of laughter, "My God!"

"Yeah, see? So, you really made me mad."

"How can I make it up to you?" she said.

"Denigrate me some more over dinner."

"No," she said, and his smile dissolved. "But I'll take you to brunch."

His eyes lit up. "Fantastic!" he said. "When, tomorrow?"

"Twelve-thirty at the Cajun Kitchen, 18th and Columbia."

"Super, I'm really looking forward to it," he said, turning away. "Hey, the house looks great," his voice fading as he approached the front door, "Do some painting, did you?"

Mondays, she cleaned the Merritt's Colonial home in Chevy Chase. This Monday, she started in on the dining room chandelier. The conventional school counseled the removal of each crystal piece to be cleaned individually at least twice a year. She didn't have that kind of time. Instead, she carefully levered the Kittinger table out of the way, laid a drop cloth on the antique Aubusson rug, then set up a high step ladder. Perched on top, she washed the crystals in place using a solution of ammonia and distilled water. Instead of newspaper, however, too unwieldy to use at close quarters, she used cheesecloth, malleable enough to work around the glass facets. The innovation had cut the time to half a day and it had been this kind of detail that garnered her the recommendations and the jobs. Of course, she had learned the trick from Juana.

As she scrubbed, she thought of Mark. The center of his universe opposed hers diametrically, she thought. But his boyish glee at things seemed so genuine to her, so pure. She had expected the brunch date to restore order to the situation, but it hadn't been so.

"You know, I've been so lucky, I must have been very good in my former life."

"Oh?" she said, bemused and perhaps a little bit happy from the Mimosa. "You believe in reincarnation?"

"Yup. I figure I was a cockroach before. No, really," he held up his hand to stem her laugh of ridicule. "I was a very successful cockroach, a giant among bugs. I met the highest standards, all the other roaches honored me because I was the first to infest San Francisco's beautiful, tony hotel, the St. Regis. True, over time the exterminators got me, but not before I laid 480,062 eggs. Naturally, this nonpareil feat never made it into human annals, because as soon as the little suckers hatched, the horrified St. Regis staff claimed that they were not cockroaches. They said they were a rare genus of African beetles introduced by some biologist, a British Lord, I believe. You know the St. Regis, only the best, of course."

After she finished laughing, he said, "So, what about you? Were you a communist in your former life, too, or just an anarchist?"

She smiled bravely, "I don't know. I'm not much of a Buddhist."

"But you are a communist."

"Sure. And someday I'm going to undo the likes of you."

"I can't wait. So, you've read all of Marx and Engels?"

"No," she said, feeling a hint of heat ascend her neck, "I never needed to. I know what the bottom line is, my father was an economist." She giggled, "My sister and I secretly called him the ecommunist because he used to make these pronouncements at the dinner table. 'This family is not a democracy, it is a communist state: from each according to his abilities, to each according to his needs.' Stuff like that."

She took another long sip of her Mimosa. "But anyway you cut it, the rich are rich at the expense of the poor. And there are many, many more who are poor." She raised a finger up in the air, "This must be fixed."

"What, the ceiling?" he said.

She laughed abruptly, then cut it short, assuming a severe, admonishing expression.

"Sorry, channeling Monty Python," he mumbled.

He sat looking at her for a time. Then he said, "I'm convinced. It hasn't been my experience, but when you're ready to redistribute the world's wealth, let me know. I'll help."

"Sure," she said with a smirk. "So, am I fired now that you know I intend to crush you?"

He looked at her askance. "Of course not. I'm Silly Putty in your hands."

He leaned over and kissed her lightly and suddenly she knew all about truth in lending.

This was how lifelong Democrats ended up marrying dyed-in-the-wool Republicans, she thought as she moved from crystal to crystal, from top to bottom. Only, this was worse, a fake repentant capitalist. So, what was she going to do when she went over there this Friday? The question had been racing in her mind throughout the weekend. Why, she didn't know, since the man did have to work during the week. The whole thing was moot, since he wouldn't even be there.

She rubbed the facet in her hand hard enough for the light coming in the tall sash windows to dance off its surface, spearing her in the eye.

"Sheila," a voice called. She blinked and looked down from the ladder. Margaret Merritt, wife of James Merritt, Esquire, gazed up at her from just inside the doorway. She wore a suit with a short skirt, one of her Adolfos, Sheila guessed. Her hands on her waist allowed the light to play tag with the chandelier crystals and her watch, the Cartier.

"So, this is how you do it," she said. "I always wondered."

She conducted a brief inspection, "But you moved the table. I hope you were careful to lift it." She turned to Sheila. "I just wanted to tell you that Jim and I definitely will be going to New York for the antique show. That will be Thursday the 4th through Friday the 5th. It would be a perfect time for you to get to the upstairs closets, don't you think?"

"I'm not sure I can do that, Mrs. Merritt. I'll have to check with my other clients to see if they mind my switching."

"But surely they'll understand, especially since you've been with us the longest."

"I can't be sure, Mrs. Merritt. I will ask, then call you."

"Oh, I hope that you can work it out. It would be so convenient."

"I'll let you know as soon as I know."

"That leaves Fridays," Leo said. "How does it look?"

"I don't know," Sheila said almost wistfully. "He didn't bring it up."

"Yeah, well, four isn't bad, Sheila. You might not want to push your luck, you know?"

"No, no, I'll find out. If there's a chance, he'll be included."

She was sitting on the windowsill outside the front bathroom on the second floor, rubbing dry the glass hexagons when she heard his car. Mark straightened up out of the driver's side, pulling his trench coat around him against the freezing cold. Then, he opened the back door and leaned in. He brought out a white cardboard box, a bunch of roses wrapped in tissue, and a bottle of white wine.

"Oh God," she moaned. She pulled herself back into the bathroom and ran into the hallway, where she stopped. This was stupid. He would put the wine in the refrigerator, the roses in water, and the rest somewhere else, go back to his car, and drive away.

"Sheila! Lunchtime!"

"You shouldn't have done this," she said, her arms folded around her. She stood on the second step of the stairs, which allowed her to look down on him with disapproval.

"You have to eat lunch, right? Well, here it is."

"And the flowers?"

"I like flowers, don't you?"

"Mr. Roth, I work for you! I am your cleaning lady."

"Hey, it was Mark on Saturday. What did I do?"

"Nothing, but that was a special, uh, a unique occasion. I'd insulted you."

"And I'm still pissed." He faux pouted, "Think of how miffed I'll be if you don't help me eat this marvelous crab salad brought all the way here from one of the finest eateries in Annapolis."

"You didn't drive all the way to Annapolis?"

"Of course not," he said smugly, "I had it couriered. But you still should be flattered that I went to all this trouble for you," he said, smiled his winning smile, "especially since I'm drop-dead good-looking." He struck his pose, and laughing, she flew off of the stairs to wrap him in her arms.

"Tell me about your other clients," he whispered to her insidiously, his head on the same pillow, his lips almost touching her ear.

"What's to know? They're all rich."

"No, really, who's who?"

"Why do you want to know this?"

"Because I'm a busybody, a gossip monger. I'm not really a banker, I'm a tabloid journalist. Inquiring minds need to know."

She rolled her eyes at him with a wry expression. "Okay. There's James Merritt, a very high-powered attorney and his wife. They live in Chevy Chase, very rich, beautiful furniture and antique rugs, Persian, and Chinese. She's a bitch with airs and thinks her collection is very good."

"Why do you hate them?"

"He lobbies for the NRA and the American Tobacco Institute."

"Ah-hah."

"Her stuff is good, a Bevan Funnell breakfront, lovely walnut, Harden dressers, and the rugs, . . . but she can't touch the Dolans."

"The Dolans?"

"A former assistant secretary in the Defense Department, now a big-time lobbyist. He has old money, from Illinois. Strictly Brooks Brothers suits and single-malt scotch. His wife wears some Ann Klein and Albert Nippon, and they have three kids, all in private schools. But their antiques are matchless, superb. Some 19th-century snuff boxes, a decent bunch of first editions, and he has a nice wine collection, too."

"Of course," Mark said, stretching, "his crimes against society are much more transparent."

"He was the first one I ever heard call the Gulf War 'The Bargain War.'"

"Ouch! And number three?"

"The Negris. A furrier. Need I say more?"

"You need not."

"And the radiologist, the Rosens."

"What the heck do you have against a radiologist?" he said, raising himself on one elbow.

"Hah! You don't know these guys. I found out about them by accident, literally," she said, growling a laugh. "A window came down on my hand one time, smashing one of my fingers. I went into the hospital for surgery and they had to pin the finger. Later on, I start getting these bills from a radiologist saying that I might get a separate bill from the hospital for X-Rays, but that theirs was a separate service. That even though I might only come in contact with the technician, that these medical doctors reviewed every X-Ray."

"Yeah? So?"

"So, my orthopedic guy would send me over for an X-Ray, then have me walk it back to him to review. These other guys never looked at my pictures!"

"Huh!"

"Yeah, and they were trying to dun me after my insurance had already paid them something."

"No shit?"

"Yup. If I hadn't happened to read the small print, I would've paid them. Now, I keep thinking of poor people with lousy insurance who get a bill like that. They start worrying about how they're going to pay it instead of whether it's a fair charge. So, I didn't pay, and they had a collection service, some doofus law firm, writing me lawsuit letters and all that. You know, 'The Terrors of the Earth!'"

"Wow."

"Eventually, their office called me, and when I explained everything, they swore that they had done reports. So, I told them to mail me copies. You know how they read? 'Finger is fractured.' And another one said, 'Appears to be a pin in the joint.' What assholes! So, to hell with radiologists."

They subsided into an uneasy silence for a time.

"That leaves me."

"Yeah," said Sheila. Again, quiet filled the air. "So, Mark," she said, turning to look at him with clear eyes, "are you going to be telling all your friends now that you're fucking the maid?"

He scowled, "Of course not. I'm going to tell them I'm fucking you," he said, grabbing her.

"You got news for me about Mr. America Fidelity?" Leo said.

"Yeah," Sheila said glumly, "he asked me to go with him to Hilton Head."

Leo's mouth opened. "Oh," he said, rubbing his chin. "You've been fraternizing with the Antichrist."

She nodded her head miserably. Leo covered her fingers with his own meaty, brown hands. "Sheila, we don't have to do this, you know? We can call it all off, the whole deal. You and I will still be friends."

"No, Leo, I have plans."

"Okay, then strike Roth from the list. He's expendable, especially if you like him."

"I don't know, Leo. Then what? Is he going to go to Asia with me, does he want to work in an AIDS clinic?"

"You don't know, maybe he does."

"Yeah, but I don't think so, Leo. He just isn't my kind of guy. Maybe that's part of what I like about him, but I hate myself for it."

And she did hate herself, for enjoying herself so much. He took her to the best restaurants, to shows at the Kennedy Center, the ballet, basketball games, and she didn't even like basketball. Yet, with him she liked it. He even had her going to a boat show with him in the middle of the week. True, she hadn't taken a weekday off in years, though it hadn't been hard, since it was a Thursday and the Negris were long gone to Miami. She did a perfunctory maintenance clean-up that morning, the kind run-of-the-mill services did regularly. Then, she left in time to join Mark driving to Annapolis for the afternoon.

For her part, she left notes around the house for him, "The People's Worker loves the Imperialistic Capitalist Pig in spite of his boot upon her neck," and the like. She also discovered herself looking in the mirror, wondering about her face, her hair.

None of this helped her reach a decision as March approached, then the end of March. She fretted and fretted, until finally she resolved to follow Leo's advice and talk to Mark, tell him about it, though not exact details. That was fair; if he balked, he couldn't hurt her or Leo.

Friday morning, she discovered him sitting at the table in the sunroom adjoining the kitchen. He had his chin cupped in his hand, and he was beating the side of his face with one finger.

"Mark? Something wrong?"

He stared up at her and she saw wild fear in his eyes.

"Sheila, I'm in big trouble."

"What? What is it?" she said, sitting next to him, putting her arms around his shoulders.

He sighed desperately and said, "The government is after me, for conspiracy bank fraud."

Sheila sat back, touched cold by his words. "What?"

"I said that the Feds are on me, they're on my case."

"Why? What did you do?"

"Nothing! Nothing at American Fidelity, anyway."

"Then what?" she said shrilly.

"I bought some stocks years ago in the MacPherson Fund. It was set up by some hedge fund guys to make money from another deal they had made—a sweetheart arrangement that paid back investors two dollars for every seven cents they invested. I knew somebody, so I got in on it, a one-time deal. Well, the hedge fund guys got indicted, so they cut a deal naming names. Now the SEC's coming after me, for God's sake."

She sat as still as she could, hoping that absolute immobility would make her disappear, not be here listening to these words.

He saw her and said, "Don't look at me like that, Sheila, it's not like that. I never screwed anybody at American Fidelity, I made money for all of my clients there, God damn it! This is just a mistake, one terribly small, terrible mistake."

She couldn't help her feelings for him and for herself. "All right, all right," she soothed as she embrace him, "All right."

They sat holding each other for hours on one of the white couches in the living room, gazing at the empty fireplace. Now and then, one would speak, but mostly they sat quietly.

"Have you ever heard the expression 'hoisted on your own petard?'" he asked.

"Sure, I guess."

"Petard is a French word. Literally it means bomb, colloquially it means fart. You're actually saying that you're being blown up by your own bomb exploding. The humor comes in when you think of being lifted by a fart, like in public. Now, here I am, hoisted on somebody else's petard." He slapped his hands to the side of his head and looked at her blankly, "I'm being blamed for someone else's fart."

Later on, she asked him, "So what will they do to you?"

"They'll take everything they can get their hands on," he replied sorrowfully. "Then they'll try to put me in jail."

Carefully, she said, "Why wait for that to happen?"

"What do you mean?"

"I mean, why sit around waiting for the government to put you through the ringer and then put you in prison?"

"What the hell else can I do? What choice do I have?"

"Do what other guys in your situation do. Get as much money together as you can and leave."

"What, you mean like Vesco? Yeah, he was swell for a while, but they grabbed his ass up eventually. Anyway, I don't have that kind of money. Which is probably why they didn't take me into custody. I have this house and a mortgage, the car with payments, the furniture, and maybe a couple of hundred thousand in investments, a few thousand in the bank. That's all I made out of the MacPherson thing."

"Well, get that. Sell everything else and split."

"Right, they'll let me put a 'For Sale' sign out front and waltz out of here with the down payment."

"Whatever, pull what you can together and go."

"And what would I do? This is my country, it's what I know. What would I do in Haiti, or whatever? What would you do if you were in my shoes?" he said with a slight edge to his voice.

She spoke in an offhanded tone, "If it were me, I'd go to somewhere like Thailand, or someplace else where the U.S. can't touch my money and help people there. That's what I would do."

"Oh, how noble."

"Yeah, well, you might think about it, Mark. Not only would you be welcome, it might make you feel better than any of the stuff you own. Listen, I have to go. I'll call you later."

On Monday, April Fools' Day, a large moving van pulled up to the

Negri's ranch house in Potomac. Sheila stood in the doorway, waiting.

"Good morning, Leo."

"How you doin', Sheila, everything good?"

"Everything's in perfect order."

"That's great. Okay, you want me to get the boys started?"

"First, our photo op, yes?"

"Sure, Sheila, if that's what you want."

Sheila, Leo, and his men stood in front of the mailbox while one of them took two photos with an old Polaroid camera. He handed the prints to Sheila, then took his place with the group while another man took two more photos.

"Two for you and two for me."

"Aw, I trust you, Sheila."

"Yeah, I know I'm being paranoid, but am I being paranoid enough? To quote a great American."

"Who's that, Frank Zappa?"

"It's still a good security measure," she replied.

They started cleaning out the house under Sheila's specific direction. They took all of the furniture and the clothes, even the Sherle Wagner bath fixtures. They left anything that either was valueless or traceable, like engraved jewelry. One of the men used the spare keys from the kitchen to start the Lincoln in the garage—the Negris had taken the Cadillac on the train—and drove it away. By noon, they had finished.

"Okay, Sheila, see you tomorrow at the, uh—"

"The Dolans.

That evening, she struggled about whether or not to call Mark late into the night, then finally went to bed.

On Tuesday, Sheila unlocked the two-point-three million-dollar Georgetown house owned by the Dolans and ushered Leo inside. She monitored carefully the removal of the two antique grandfather clocks, the tea table, and the Chippendale recreations. Then, she rested with

Leo while the others put the Century and other furniture into the truck.

"Did you call him?" asked Leo.

"No," she said, paging through a first edition of John Todhunter poetry. Three men filed by, each carrying a bicycle over one shoulder.

"You should call him, Sheila."

"Why would I call him? He's a shit, Leo."

"You should call him because of how you feel, Sheila. It isn't too late," he said as he climbed into Timothy Dolan's Jaguar. He drove off followed by one of his men in Mrs. Dolan's Mercedes station wagon.

But she didn't call that night, though she felt that she might bite through her lip from holding off. He didn't call her, either.

Wednesday, the 3rd of April, Leo's men emptied out Dr. Elliot Rosen's home. Sheila supervised the men as they wrapped up Mrs. Rosen's collection of crystal.

"Gorham wine glasses, Baccarat, Waterford, of course, Galway, very nice. Wedgewood China, and here's some settings by Tiffany's and Cartier. Here's a piece by Juan Quezada, one of my personal favorites. See the pattern? Stunning."

"That's a black pot, Sheila."

"You see these little fruits, Leo?" she said, holding one up.

"Yeah? Wax?"

"Ceramic. Three hundred, twenty-six dollars, and seventy-five cents apiece."

"Jesus! Hey, you guys, wrap them up carefully."

"That's nothing, Leo. This handsome bowl," she said, lifting it upside down on her fist to show him, "is an Ettore Sottass, worth ten thousand. By the way, so's the black pot."

"Excuse me, Sheila, but do you mind if I take it off of your hands?" he said, cradling the crystal after gently wresting it from her. "Thank you. You sure know a lot about this stuff, Sheila. Where did you learn it all?"

"Antique shows. Window shopping. Reading magazines, *HG*, *Architectural Digest*, and catalogs from Bloomingdales, Neiman Marcus, like that. And, of course, a lot of my clients were just tickled to tell me themselves how much their lovely, wonderful things were worth."

She leaned against empty shelves where the crystal and pottery had been displayed.

"It took a lot of work to set this up, Leo. First, I had to learn how to clean like nobody else. Then I had to find the right households, you know, the optimal opportunities. Sometimes, just when I was close, they'd hire a live-in from El Salvador, the bastards. But most of them don't want a stranger living in their house. And I had to find you, too, you know? Someone I could trust, someone who could handle the goods, too. It took a lot of time, five years."

"Whew," he said. "I can see why you're behind on your thesis. Say, what was that on again?"

"The Significance of Time in the English Novel."

"Oh yeah."

The doorbell rang, and everyone froze. Sheila said, "Okay, everybody just keep on working, business as usual."

She went to the front door and met a young woman. She brought her into the foyer, and they chatted for a few minutes, laughing and talking, their heads bobbing as they listened to each other. The woman left upon an exchange of warm good-byes.

"The babysitter, dropping off some information about day camps," said Sheila. "I've met her before. I told her that Dr. Rosen and his wife had arranged for the house to be repainted while they were in Chicago. Easier to move all the furniture out, which I'm supervising."

"You're quick on your feet, Sheila. Think she bought it?"

Sheila shrugged, "How much longer are we here?"

"An hour."

"Well," she said, "I'm game if you are."

An hour later, the truck left without incident, towing Mrs. Rosen's Volvo behind. Leo led the way in Dr. Rosen's prize Corvette, the black Quezada pot carefully packed in a box beside him on the passenger seat.

Sheila decided that she felt the greatest pleasure when she watched the Merritt's belongings file past her into the truck, especially the Kittinger table, the Aubusson rug, and the antique chandelier. She was sure to point out the value of the Modersahn and Machensen paintings to Leo, which he swore he could move into new homes. At the end of each day she had given him a complete inventory of everything they'd taken and their estimated value. Then they would dicker over price until they reached an agreement.

"I'd say we have about ten point six million worth, Sheila. By the time I find it all new homes, I'll see about forty, forty-five percent on that, out of which you get forty. So, you're looking at anywhere between four and a quarter, four and three quarters mil. That's without a contribution from Mr. Roth, by the way."

They sat in the backroom of the Arlington World Value Pawn Shop amid a number of accordions and saxophones. Leo waited, but when she didn't reply, he mumbled, "So, uh, did you try to call him, yet?"

"Nope."

"Sheila, why are you being so tough? You like the guy, what difference does it make what he did? You like me, don't you, and look at what I'm doing. Hell, Sheila, look at what you're doing. I know you're a communist and all, but shit, Sheila, you're a thief, too. You know that? So why are you being so hard on him?"

She didn't know. She couldn't answer Leo, and it bothered her all the way home. By the time she pulled up to her apartment building, she'd made up her mind. When the elevator stopped at her floor, she bounded for her door. Sure enough, her phone was ringing. She fumbled with the key, jammed it into the lock and raced across the room, the door bouncing against the jam after her. The ringing stopped. No caller ID, and no message.

"God!" she wailed.

She called all night but received no answer. Between calls, she tried Leo and asked him if he had called her earlier, but he hadn't. Then she called Mark again, and again. He's gone to Hilton Head, she thought, to put his troubles away for a week at least. Without her, she thought, because of the little sympathy she had given him.

Finally, in the middle of the night, she stopped calling. Instead, she wrote him a letter, explaining everything and leaving him an address. She would drop it off at his house tomorrow, and he could decide. There still was a chance, she thought, sleepless through the night.

On Friday morning, she popped out of a taxi on the corner of his street. She walked three blocks to his drive. Leo and the truck were already there, parked on the curb just outside the driveway. Leo got out of the truck to meet her.

"Where's the Bug?"

"I sold it. It paid for my plane ticket."

Leo smiled sadly, "You're so on it, Sheila."

"Yeah," she said, hurrying to the front of the house. "Ready?"

She pushed the key into the lock as Leo called to her, "Sheila," and she flung the door open.

The vestibule was bare. The table was gone, the mirror. She went into the living room and found it empty. She didn't bother going to any other room.

Leo stood in the doorway, his head down for her.

"You knew?"

"I peeked in the window. I thought he might be here, and I could suggest to him that you two talk things over, maybe."

"He took my advice," she said, gazing past Leo's head.

In the back room of the Pawn Shop, Leo handed Sheila an

envelope.

"There it is, two hundred and fifty big ones. The rest will go into your account in due time. If not, use your photos."

"Ah, Leo, I know I won't need those pictures."

"Yeah. You got a lot of money coming to you, Sheila, but not enough for a lifetime. And you're really gonna put it all in an AIDS clinic?"

She shook her head, "I've always had enough tucked away for myself, too, Leo," she said, poking his arm, "My father was an ecommunist, remember?"

"Yeah, yeah," he said. "And the guy?"

She sighed, "I'm going where I planned, Leo. Maybe I'll run into him. We'll be traveling in the same circles now, you know?"

"Yeah, that could be true."

"Take care of yourself, Leo."

She hugged him, kissed him on the cheek, and walked away to the waiting cab.

Richard's Play

"What is Employee-of-the-Month going to get you, Sweetcakes?" Woodall asked him, her feet propped on his desk, her hands tucked comfortably behind her neck. Richard did his best to keep his eyes on hers, not the considerable length of leg revealed by her rather unladylike posture.

"I have my reasons," he said.

"Right, right," she responded with a yawn. "A good canvass record keeps them from suggesting a different line of work, but let's face it, going where the players play makes the difference. That's where the big scores come from."

"Yeah, yeah, I know," he said as he punched out another number to try another cold call. "Hello, Dr. Roberts? I'm Richard Fontana with Able Matthews? I have a prime class-A property that's just come up at an unbelievable—" and like the others, Dr. Roberts hung up after mumbling something about not being a prospect. He dialed again.

Woodall preferred to work the reception circuit, American Fidelity's quarterly financial forecast gig, Feingold's reelection soiree, anything where people with sizable growth might show up. She was right about the personal contacts, and she did all right, better than all right. Of course, he didn't have satiny black hair sweeping down to his coccyx or a killer bod and a beautiful face to go with it all. Not that he was bad looking. Even at six feet in a suit, his blue eyes and blond hair gave him a boyish charm, or at least so said Woodall. But he knew better than to vie with her in that arena. No, he had to work hard to get ahead of the others in the bullpen, and he was willing to do it.

"So, you're Employee-of-the-Month. Oh, it's a nice little honor and all, but do you really think it means shit to Ebersole? He could care so much. As long as you make the moves, fine. But otherwise, what's the big deal?"

Richard didn't bother to answer.

"Okay, you tell me what it means."

He turned his head to her, wearing a secret little grin. "Promise not to tell? You know, Andy and the others?"

She smiled an enigma of her own, dropped her legs and leaned toward him with a shake of her hair. "Why, Richard, of course."

"Okay." He put the receiver in its cradle and opened the top drawer of his desk. He slipped out a piece of paper and handed it to Woodall.

She started reading, then said, "What's this?"

"What you get when you're the Employee of the Month."

"What, a parking space next to the president? You're kidding? When did this start?"

"This month. As an incentive. They posted it a few weeks ago. I, uh, kind of annexed the announcement."

"Jesus Christ, Fontana, you larcenous bastard. And you think this is going to put you ahead? A parking spot next to Kistler? Dream on, Loverboy."

She stood up and started long strides out of the office.

"Yeah, well, we'll see tomorrow," he muttered.

In the morning, he drove his car tentatively into the parking garage. Instead of barreling down the ramp to the third level as usual, this time he cruised on street level slowly past the fire lane toward a row of open spots. At the head of each space a sign bore the name of the executive who parked there. Richard passed each one in turn, Readmon, V.P. of Finance; Ennunzio, V.P., Sales; Brennan, Public Affairs; Lentz, V.P. of Marketing; Malloy, Exec. V.P.; and Kistler, President and C.E.O.

He had to back up. Kistler, Malloy, — there it was, an open space. Above the long, yellow concrete block was a new sign bolted into the wall.

Fontana

Holy shit. They even went to the trouble of bolting in a name plate for just one month. He pulled his car into the space, turned off the engine, and sat for a moment. Someday he would make this his permanent space. That would keep Woodall from laughing. It might even make her come around maybe.

He stepped out of the car gingerly. He looked up and down the lane and watched a few cars drive in. A Mercedes took the far spot. Readmon. The graying man nodded pleasantly as he headed for the building entrance. In his mid-fifties, Richard thought, though he could be wrong. Extra weight made you look older. Richard vowed to himself he would be a V.P. before he was fifty, and he would never let himself go to pot.

A couple of other cars passed by on their way to the lower levels. Richard turned back for his briefcase. He smiled a bit sheepishly. Even though he'd washed and waxed it yesterday afternoon, a five-year old Ford was still a Ford.

"Well, how's your power parking working out, Fontana?"

"Huh?"

Richard looked up from his desk into Andy Cosigliani's tan face framed in his perfect black hair. Woodall sat at her desk, alert, watching expectantly.

"You know, park with the honchos, be a honcho."

"What're you talking about?"

"Woodall told me. You know, about the bulletin you lifted."

Richard shot her an ugly look and she smiled innocently, opening her hands to him.

"So, how many heart-to-hearts do you think you and Kistler will have?" Cosigiliani went on.

"It'll be just fine," said Richard.

"Sure it will. Only, don't you remember? This is the month Kistler spends in St. Croix in his condo."

Shit! That's right. Goddamn it, he thought, he'd completely forgotten.

"You be riding de ferry down to de Islands, Mon, to take full advantage of your parking privileges?"

"It doesn't matter, Cosigliani, a lot of heavy hitters park in that row. And I'll win the spot again next month, too, so it doesn't matter that Kistler isn't here."

"Fat chance, Buddy Boy. We're on to you, now. Enjoy what you can while you can."

He didn't, much. After the novelty wore off, he had to admit that the space was just about the same as any other. He saw plenty of the officers, but they all just nodded pleasantly, smiling as they proceeded up to their posh offices while he headed into the bullpen. By the end of the week he didn't give it another thought, except at the end of the day when he peeled off from the others on the first level while they walked into the bowels of the garage. That was kind of nice.

On Friday, Richard loosened his tie and fished in his jacket for his keys. It was late, and he figured to head on home and go directly to bed. He would be back in the morning to do paperwork that had been ignored while he'd been hitting the phones.

As he strolled down the stained concrete floor closing in on his space, the car next to his lurched violently backwards and he heard the sound of a metal-wrenching crash.

"Hey," he yelled, half-trotting to his car. The other vehicle eased forward. "What the hell?"

Richard looked at the ripped rear fender of his car, torn open by the bumper of the Cadillac on the right.

"Jesus Christ!" he cried out, "look what you did to my car!"

A heavy man with thinning gray hair on an enormous head stepped out of the Cadillac. He wore a full white beard and thick glasses. His suit, although expensive looking, was rumpled as though he was wearing it for the second straight day.

"Sorry. Pretty tight fit, these garage spaces."

"Are you nuts?" Richard said leaning over his destroyed fender. "You had plenty of room." He ran an index finger over a newly torn ragged blade of metal, "What're you, drunk or something?"

"Now, look. I just didn't see your car. Here. Here's my insurance company. Tell them Terry Brennan gave you this. I'll call my agent."

Richard came to himself. "Oh. Yeah. Okay, Mr. Brennan."

"Okay. You okay?" the wide man asked. "Okay. I'm sorry."

He backed the Cadillac out slowly and drove off.

"Fuck," Richard mumbled. He surveyed the damage over and over again, his hands on his hips.

"That's a shame," a voice said from a few cars down.

"Tell me about it. How could he do that? Man, you could've backed an elephant out of there with the room I left."

"That is a shame. Your fender is bent almost into the wheel. Are you sure you can drive it?"

"Hell, I don't know."

Richard leaned over and grabbed the bent fender, careful to avoid the torn part, and pulled. The crimped metal gave way.

"Well, I guess I can drive it."

"That's good. Who hit you?"

For the first time Richard noticed who was talking to him. Alden Malloy, Executive V.P. of Able Matthews.

"Uh, Brennan, Mr. Brennan."

"Brennan, huh? Darn shame."

Malloy cut a mean figure in his dark pinstripe. Straight up and down he was, probably a skinny guy in a bathing suit. But in corporate battle gear, he was a killer, especially with that wavy brown hair just touched with gray, like racing stripes. Now this was the way to age gracefully, thought Richard.

"You're Richard Fontana, right?"

"Why, yes, Mr. Malloy."

"In Ebersole's group?"

"Yessir. I'm the Employee of the Month." As soon as the words came out, he wanted to throw himself under the wheels of the nearest passing car.

"Yes, yes, I know. That's very good. Ebersole's got a good group. Well. Have a nice weekend. And I hope the car works out all right."

"Right. Thanks. Good night."

So, maybe it hadn't turned out like he'd imagined it would. Meeting Malloy wasn't too shoddy. But that asshole Brennan had to wreck my car, he thought.

On Monday, he walked into the bullpen late. He'd had to take the bus into work and wasn't used to the schedule. He'd missed the first one.

"Hey, Richard, where've you been?" asked Woodall. "You'll never repeat as Employee of the Month at this rate."

"Yeah, yeah."

"I hear you dinged your car, Fontana. That kind of puts a crimp, if you know what I mean, in your master parking plan for world domination, doesn't it?"

"Kiss off, Cosigliani."

Cosigliani pursed his lips and smacked them several times.

"Bad luck, Richard," said Woodall.

"Yeah," Richard replied absently as he picked up the note on his desk. "Hey. Malloy wants to see me. How about that shit?" he said, mugging at Cosigliani as he went out the door.

On the eleventh floor of the Matthews Building, Richard walked out of the elevator and quickly padded down the deep, fisherman green pile carpeting covering the light lime-green, Italian marble floor. He headed toward the rosewood doors at the end of the corridor. Before he reached the two with the brass plate that proclaimed Kistler's office, he faced right and knocked on the varnished panel of a single door labeled Malloy.

After a full minute, the door opened partially and a gorgeous young woman peered around it and said, "Yes? You can come inside."

"Oh," Richard said softly, and he reddened slightly as he passed by her into the large reception area. Two other women sat at desks typing between answering telephones.

"Can I help you?"

"Uh, yeah, Mr. Malloy asked me to come see him."

She smiled brilliantly, politely waiting. "And you are?"

"Fontana. Richard Fontana."

"Okay, just a minute."

She returned to her seat behind a desk perpendicular to the doorway and dialed her phone.

"Go right in."

"Hello, Richard," said Malloy coming from behind his desk.
"How are you? How's the car?"

"Good, good. Okay. It's at the shop right now."

"Unhuh. What's the prognosis?"

"Full recovery," he said, beaming a smile.

"Oh. that's great, excellent news. Here, have a seat."

Richard sat in one of the Queen Anne chairs in front of Malloy's huge mahogany desk. One piece of paper occupied the suede leather blotter in the middle, along with one brass lamp.

"You know, that was a shame about Terry and your car. I can't imagine how it happened."

"Neither can I. You can fit a Bradley tank in those spots. He must have done some amazing steering to rap my car like that."

"Yes, well, you don't think anything was wrong, do you? I mean, with him?"

Richard drew his head back ever so slightly. "What do you mean?"

Malloy folded his hands on top of the paper, making Richard wonder idly if he had placed it on the blotter just for that purpose, to keep him from marking the suede. Or, maybe it was the other way around, to keep from dulling his gold cufflinks.

"Oh, I just wondered if things have been getting to Terry—Mr. Brennan these days. His wife died a few years ago you know, and they'd been married for quite some time. Then, he went through two other marriages that didn't last very long. He's been through some very tough moments, emotionally speaking."

"Is that right? I didn't know that."

"Yes. His health hasn't been great. Terry's a good guy, he's done some terrific work for Able Matthews over the past twenty years. But it takes its toll. In Public Affairs, you know, you have to do quite a bit of entertaining."

"You do?"

"Yes. Lunches with the media. A lot of receptions. It can be hard on the body."

"Unhuh."

"I guess that's why when he banged your car, you said something, I thought, 'Well—"

"I said something?"

"Yes, something about why you thought he might have hit your car."

"I said he was nuts?" Richard said, "Or maybe drunk."

"Yes," Malloy said distantly. "Listen, would you do me a favor? Would you mind talking with a friend of mine? Her name is Dottie Burns. She's a psychological consultant for the company. She might have some questions about Terry Brennan that maybe you could help her with."

"Why, I'd be happy to, Mr. Malloy."

"Fine, excellent. So, Richard, how long have you been with the company, a year?"

"A little over. Eighteen months."

"And how are things going? They must be going well, you're the Employee of the Month."

"It's going all right. I've made a few deals, 5,000 feet here, 10,000 there. Nothing big."

He'd never made a 10,000-foot deal, not to one client, but it didn't hurt to exaggerate a bit, he figured.

"Yeah, it's tough," said Malloy. "Especially in the middle of the worst recession in real estate history. You know, sometimes it's just a matter of getting together with the right people to make the right match. Let me make a phone call, see if we can't do something together."

"That would be great, Mr. Malloy!"

"Call me Alden."

Richard met with Dottie Burns in her office on the tenth floor. He didn't bother with the elevator. As he skittered down the fire stairs, he laughed wryly to himself that he was working his way down the corporate ladder.

"It's very good to see you, Richard," she said, shaking his hand quite warmly. "Mr. Malloy says you had a run-in with Mr. Brennan?"

"I'll say!" he said ingenuously, and he let loose a burst of laughter.

"How did this happen?" she said. She looked to be thirty something, with frizzy hair and a layered style, a Cardigan sweater over a blouse and skirt. Not bad looking, but no movie star.

"Jeez, I don't know. I was walking to my car, and it looked like Brennan—Mr. Brennan—just turned his car into mine. I couldn't figure out how he could have done it."

"Did you have words?"

"Well, I told him he must be crazy, either that or drunk."

"Do you think he had been drinking?"

"Gee, I don't know. I was leaving late, but it was still early evening, only about six-thirty."

"Did you smell alcohol on his breath when you talked?"

"No, not that I remember."

"I see," she said, spinning a pencil eraser down on her desk. The desktop was covered with little mementos, photo frames, and some flowers that looked to be a day or two old.

"Did you by any chance see any cigarette burns on his car seat?"

"To tell you the truth, Ms. Burns, I didn't get anywhere near his front seat. I spent most of the time looking at my rear fender."

"Sure, sure, certainly. Was he in any way hostile?"

"No, no, he was pretty calm. He gave me a card for his insurance, you know, his agent, told me to use his name. Almost like this had happened to him before. More than once."

"Uh-huh. Richard, I want to thank you for coming to see me. You've been an enormous help."

"Hey, my pleasure."

Weird woman, he thought as he descended to the bullpen.

The word drifted down in a matter of days.

"Did you hear about Brennan?" Woodall said. "He's gone. Off to the Huntsdale Clinic. You know what that is? Corporate America's answer to Betty Ford."

"No shit!" said Cosigliani. "You're kidding!"

"I am not kidding. I talked with Jennifer up in Public Affairs. She said Malloy came in and made an announcement to the entire department that Brennan was going to a psychiatric clinic for his health and that they should not expect to see him for 29 days."

"Get the hell out!" cried Cosigliani. He jumped up, clicked his heels together and snapped his right hand into the air. "I vill follow you anywhere, mien fuhrer. Sieg heil!"

"Il Duce to you, Andy."

As Richard listened to the news, he grew smaller and smaller in his seat. He already had his car back, good as new with a fresh wax job. It hadn't cost him a cent. Well, a phone call from Malloy might make him feel better. He waited for the phone call, but it didn't come, not over the next three weeks. In the meantime, more details filtered down about Brennan, of how Burns had confronted him with the decision about the clinic, and how they had left on the spot without even telling his kids, not even the one still living at home. Rumor had it that Brennan's expense accounts were way out of line and that Malloy at one time had exploded, yelling that Brennan better have a drinking problem because if he didn't, then his poor work record would stand alone at the office. Brennan's medical records reportedly evidenced a lot of liver damage.

Richard began to lose interest as his own problems closed in on him. He made call after call, hit the streets, tried prospect after prospect, but made no headway. He even resorted to calling clients with whom he'd just closed deals to see if they needed to expand. Nothing. The market was lousy, he thought, there was so much space out there, including prime stuff in Loudoun County, and right downtown in the CBD. How was a guy supposed to win? Even Woodall appeared grim-faced these days, though she seemed to have a lock on Employee of the Month for next month. He would have to give up his now-beloved parking space. This made him feel even lousier. He consoled himself only by knowing that Cosigliani was really sucking on the tailpipe. Tomorrow was the last day of the month. He had to have something, anything, or he might be in real jeopardy. Sighing, he reached for the phone.

It rang before he could lift it off the hook.

"Richard Fontana? Yes, I'm Maurice Gettinger of Horowitz, Renault, O'Rourke and Amalda. I've been talking to Mr. Malloy about our expansion plans and he suggested that I call you to arrange an appointment to discuss some possibilities."

Warmth began to flow through Richard's veins from his feet to the top of his head.

"Why, I'd be happy to, Mr. Gettinger. Let me take down some

details. Uh, how much space are you occupying at present?"

"Oh, about 22,000 square feet. We calculate a need for about double that, maybe more."

Richard stood straight up in his seat, threw his eyes skyward, and mouthed, 50,000 square feet!

"But Alden has all this information," Gettinger went on, "He just wants you to meet me. You know, talk about some locations, narrow them down to a few select choices before we bring in the senior partners. Mr. Malloy found us our current space and we were quite pleased with the results."

"Well, I'm sure we can do that, Mr. Gettinger. We'll get right to it."

"Call me Maurice."

"Yessir. And you certainly can call me Richard."

He won Employee of the Month going away, the second consecutive month, a new record, since there hadn't been any before. Woodall pouted, but allowed him to take her to lunch as a peace offering. They ate at the Old Ebbet's Grill, her choice. But he felt flush, with the big lease looking like a sure thing even if he did have to share the commission with Malloy. To the lion goes the lion's share, he said to himself.

"So, have you heard the latest in the Brennan soap?"

"No," he said sullenly. "We don't have to go over that again, do we?"

"Ah, but a new twist," said Woodall. Her eyes flashed a knowing glint over her Virgin Mary. "Kistler's back in town, you know."

"Yes," he said grinning broadly, "I saw him in the parking garage this morning."

"All right, mister, don't rub it in," she admonished. "Well, here's the thing. Word has it that Kistler didn't know anything about Brennan being spirited off to Huntsdale."

"Oh?"

"That's right."

"Huh." Richard fumbled with his drink, a Saratoga with a twist. "So, what do you think that means?"

"Oh, I don't know," she said in a flighty singsong. "But there it is."

"Yeah," he said, sucking up air against the ice in the bottom of his glass.

He waited for something to happen, but nothing seemed awry. Malloy had cut him in on a nearly done deal with the law firm. Just for doing a little legwork, he saw the papers signed and a big commission for himself assured. So, that looked good. And he had seen Kistler a couple of times in the parking lot. The old man, with his giant bushy eyebrows, had nodded at him pleasantly and wished him a good day.

At the beginning of his second week of his second term as Employee of the Month, his immediate boss Ebersole called him into his office.

"Richard, I got a favor I want to ask for you to do." Ebersole came from New York and he talked like it. In fact, he looked it, which always brought on conjecture about how could he possibly get to know the people he leased space to unless he was connected.

"What's that, Charlie?"

"Look, Terry Brennan's in the Huntsdale Clinic, right? Right. Well, he's getting out early, tomorrow morning. He has no way of getting home. He needs a ride."

"Me?"

"His kid's gotta work and I can't leave here. I would appreciate it as a personal favor."

"Me?"

"You can go to his house, pick up his Caddy, and drive him back. No problem about the time. I'll take care of it."

"Aw, Charlie, why me?"

Ebersole looked at him coldly. "Why you? Why not you? I could of given this to Cosigliani or Woodall, any of them out there. I consider this a personal favor." He stressed the last word.

"Yeah, but Charlie—"

"Yeah but what?"

From his house to Brennan's to Huntsdale, Maryland, Richard fretted. How could he face this guy? Then again, he thought, what difference did it make, he didn't know Brennan, really. But, damn, he was a vice president! Shit!

He drove up a broad, curving macadam road to a complex of two-story brick buildings surrounded by green lawns, tennis courts, and swimming pools. He was surprised there was no golf course.

Brennan stood at the entrance with one small leather suitcase at his side. He appeared smaller to Richard. He'd probably lost weight, Richard thought, being off the booze. He wore a flannel shirt open at the collar, a blue woolen CPO shirt over it, khaki slacks, and boat moccasins. On his head he wore a Swedish fisherman's cap.

Richard got out of the car and walked around to take Brennan's suitcase.

"Hi, Richard, how are you doing?"

"Hello, Mr. Brennan, fine, fine . . .." He awkwardly shook hands after switching the suitcase over to his left.

"How's the car?"

"Oh, uh, good, good. How are you? You look good."

"I'm okay. Well rested. Shall we go?"

"Sure, sure."

They started out on Route 9 toward the Interstate.

"So, what's new back at the ranch?" asked Brennan.

Richard kept his eyes on the road. "Nothing much. The market stinks, but what's new about that?"

"Right, right. And how is everybody? How's Charlie?"

"Okay, he's good."

"Unhuh. And Malloy?"

Richard chanced a sidelong glance. He couldn't see anything behind those thick glasses. Brennan had removed his hat, and a wisp of gray hair hung over his forehead. He pushed it back with his hand.

"Well, he's good, I think. I don't see much of him where I am."

"But I heard you and he just did a sizable deal together."

Richard shifted in his seat. "How did you hear that?"

"Oh, Charlie told me. He told me that Malloy did an able job filling in for me, too."

"Unhuh."

"Well, that's good. I've known him for a long time, you know."

"Really?"

"Oh, yeah," said Brennan, "Way before Able Matthews. You know, I wasn't always in Public Affairs. I used to be an economist."

"Is that right?"

"Yup. With Met Ed way back in the sixties. Back before you were born, I'll bet. And Malloy was there, too."

"Yeah?"

"Sure. He was in charge of development. He and I were there when they were planning the Shackleford Power Plant, remember that?"

"No, I don't," Richard said. He could feel sweat dripping down the inside of his shirt from his armpits. Why? he asked himself, Brennan wasn't saying anything about him. He probably doesn't even know. Then, why am I driving him back? he wondered.

"Yeah. Malloy came into the meeting with blueprints, engineers, the whole shebang. That's his style, all right. Elan. And the plans were good, very good, state-of-the-art, top of the line. Trouble was, the plant only burned oil."

"Oh," Richard said solemnly, not knowing at all what Brennan was talking about.

"Yes. You see, as the economist, I had to do resource models. And, in my position I had an obligation to advise the company to build the plant with the dual capacity to burn both oil and coal."

"Huh," Richard said as he turned onto the Interstate.

"Right. Well, they went oil. Then the crisis of 1973 happened. You remember that?"

"Afraid I don't, Mr. Brennan."

"Yeah, well. Shackleford was about half-done, but they couldn't change it at that point. It was soon after that when Malloy got into the commercial real estate business."

"I get you," Richard said. "And when did you come to Able Matthews, Mr. Brennan?" Try a new tack, he thought, redirect the conversation.

"Oh, shortly after that. Met Ed wasn't all that happy with me about Shackleford, either. You know, Cassandra, the bearer of bad news and all that. Of course, she was a woman. I wonder if there's a male counterpart to her somewhere in Greek mythology. They usually did that."

Richard darted glances over, wondering if he was driving with a crazy man sitting next to him.

"Anyway, Met Ed dealt me out. I was lucky that Kistler asked me to come to Able Matthews, though it sure did surprise the hell out of Malloy. Yeah, Met Ed used booze as an excuse, which probably inspired Malloy. Oh yeah, ever since he left Met Ed in a hurry, Malloy has had it in for me. But he had to wait for me to screw up enough to be able to get me himself. And, let's face it, Richard, I've punished the bottle over the years and now it's punishing me."

Richard relaxed somewhat. It sounded as though Brennan had no inkling.

"So, the rest did me good, you know, and I'm sure that my liver is in better shape. But, man, there are a lot of sick guys in that place. Really sick, you know what I mean? They have them on a whole host of drugs—diazepam, that's to stop the shakes, and Librium, some on Thorazine, reserpine, chlorpromazine, aspirin, and vitamin B-12. Quite a regimen," he said.

"Sounds like it," Richard said.

"Oh, yeah. And they take away your belt and shoelaces, you know? They don't want you to get depressed and kill yourself. And here I thought it was the booze that depressed you.

"Yeah," Brennan continued, "It's like a police state, a soft police state. You know how they came to take me? Dottie Burns told me that they thought I was an alcoholic. This is after she's had lunch with me, where she's asking me if other people in my department have drinking problems. I said we all do, collectively. You see, that is how they work, putting together this ticky-tacky shit. Innuendo and the like. Then she confronts you with her professional opinion and says they've made the arrangements. All based on this circumstantial shit."

Richard did not like the timbre of Brennan's voice or where he was headed at all. "Yeah, well, it's all over now, Mr. Brennan."

"Like a cigarette burn in my front seat, for Christ sake. She said it could have come from me being out of control, driving while drinking. A cigarette burn, for Christ sake!"

Oh shit, thought Richard.

"And a fender bender. She says I can't drive because I'm drinking. Look at my glasses, for God's sake. I can't drive because I can't see!"

He held the glasses in front of Richard's face. Richard glanced at them, at the road, then at them again. His own eyes were wide open, and his mouth hung open as well.

"What does she do, that bitch? She talks to people, asking those witch-hunting questions, you know, those character-assassination specials. Like 'Why do you think he 'drove into your car?' And they answer her by saying, 'He must have been drunk.'"

"Shit!" Richard shouted.

"Shit is right, you little shit! Did you think you were going to get away with this? Did you think you could match dicks with me?"

"Oh, fuck," moaned Richard.

"Oh, fuck is right because you are fucked! Do you really think

Malloy will survive this? I will eviscerate him! They didn't even let me call my kid!"

"Mr. Brennan—"

"Shut up. You think because Malloy's the executive vice president it makes a difference in the pecking order? Well, my fine boyo, who do you think called me up at Huntsdale to arrange to have a drink as soon as I'm back? None other than Ernest T. Kistler himself."

"Oh my God," whimpered Richard.

"Right. Malloy never would have pulled this stunt with Kistler in town. But he's feeling his oats because Kistler's ready to retire. Well, not yet."

"Jesus, Jesus, Jesus!"

"That's right, Laddy, pray, pray hard."

They drove along in brooding silence. Richard felt himself near to tears of fear. There goes my job, there goes my parking space, he mourned, if he doesn't kill me first.

"Oh, don't mope, kid, I'm not going to kill you. This is the Irish Mafia, we don't murder people, we get even. But these things have to be done delicately, my pretty, to quote a grand old lady. And how to do it, how to hoist Malloy from the nearest yardarm?"

Richard saw a dim light glowing.

"That's right, Fontana, you've suffered enough for being such a minor shit in this play. You think that's the only reason I told Charlie to send you? No, kid, you've proven yourself to be a real useful fucking guy. So, relax."

Saved! he thought. I'm saved!

"And Fontana, remember this. I know changing loyalty doesn't come cheap. Remember, between me, Charlie, and Kistler, we know a lot of people. There are a million deals to be done, a million of them. Yeah, I can see it in you, kid. You've got the makings of one hell of a Malloy, I can see it in your eyes. Hey, keep them on the road."

For the first time since he had gotten up that morning, Richard smiled. Kistler, Brennan, and Ebersole, all cutting him in—he'd be rich! Woodall would go to lunch with him; hell, she'd might even go to bed with him! And, he thought warmly, he could keep his parking space for a while longer, maybe even forever.

He couldn't keep from smiling to himself all the way back.

City Mouse, Country Mouse

Straightening up out of the cab, Karen was surprised to see a mass of girders and steel instead of a regular building. She frowned and turned back to the cabdriver. "Is this the right place, the address I gave you?"

He looked at the slip of paper, then craned his neck out of the window. "Yeah, check the sign. See there? One Thousand Fourth Street, Northwest. Looks like it isn't quite finished yet."

She gazed around at the dilapidated row houses surrounding the area, at the small park across the street where a lone figure shot baskets at a single backboard, then back at the steel framework where William Caso's office was supposed to be.

"Now what do I do?"

"Look up," said the driver, again awkwardly sticking his head and shoulders out the window.

She peered up at the structure and noticed that part at the top had walls around it and light in the windows.

"You don't think anyone's up there, do you?"

The driver, thirtyish, wearing one of those Irish newsboy caps over one eye, shrugged and said, "The sign says this is a Caso job. He's kind of an iconoclastic guy, so the papers say." He shrugged again.

She glanced at him and said wryly, "Iconoclastic?"

He feigned indignation, "Hey, I have a dictionary."

She laughed, looked up again, then scanned the neighborhood once more. "Do you think you could stay around for a while until I come back?"

He'd shifted back behind the wheel and seemed not to be paying attention as he muttered, "It might could be arranged." He said it not looking at her, but at the park and the player driving to the basket, laying in the ball.

"Okay. I'll be right back. Twenty minutes. I won't be long."

"I'll be here," he said distractedly.

Karen followed a path that wove between a giant crane, piles of sand, portable concrete mixers, scraps of wood, slim rusted iron rods, concrete-encrusted pails, and other evidence of work in progress. Inside, she passed over a concrete floor, greenish in color that looked almost soft. At the end of the path, she arrived at shiny, stainless steel elevator doors shrouded in plastic. The interior of the elevator was covered with cardboard, but she could see the edges of deep, rich, maroon wooden panels peeking out between the seams.

The elevator shot her up to the top floor, the thirteenth, she was surprised to see. She stepped out into the hallway and immediately thought that never again could she expect to see so much pink marble in one place. Following a path cut through the dust on the polished stone floor, she made her way to two brass double doors, both partially open. She walked in. Behind a ten-foot oval desk with slender chrome legs and a wooden top stained a deep reddish black sat a dark-haired man.

He wore an impeccably tailored suit, a double-breasted Italian cut made of worsted wool. He was talking into a phone, but as soon as he saw her, he motioned her in. Covering the mic, he said, "Hi, Karen. You are Karen? Great, please take a seat, I'll only be a minute."

She sat in a burnt-orange leather chair, and while he talked, allowed herself to take in the elegant couches and chairs, the polished marble end tables, the deep jade vases, the crystal lamps with contemporary white linen shades, and the glow of the richly colored walls and cabinets.

She looked at him, dark-haired and handsome in a classical sort of way. He gestured with one hand as he spoke into the thin black receiver.

"Earl," he said, "I can't do that, Earl. That is non-doable, it is something I cannot do. We've been over this. I can't make the numbers work with a 5.5 FAR, I need a 10. They can't expect me to give them a childcare center and also ante up a homeless shelter for a measly 5.5. It just doesn't compute, I might as well sell. No. No, density elsewhere does me no good. Earl, you know how much that piece of ground cost? I need that 10. For my investors to have any chance to see their money again, I need 500,000 square feet. No, I don't want to meet with them, not until we can agree. It's not workable with both the childcare center and the homeless shelter," he paused, then began to burble laughter, "unless we combine them. Yeah, have the homeless babysit the kids. Simple, kill two social problems with one stone."

He roared laughter, infectious laughter, she realized, as he went on to say, "I know, I know, I'm terrible. It's an evil thought and I'm contrite now. But talk to him, Earl, talk their language to them. Yes, I know he's running for office again, soon, but they're always running for office."

He waited, listening. And waited. As the wait lengthened, she thought she heard something bizarre; he had started to hum very softly, "You are my sunshine, my only sunshine. You make me happy when skies are gray—Earl, I'll meet with them when you're closer, okay? Okay. Bye, take care."

He cradled the receiver, then sighed. "Lawyers. Can't live with them, can't sue without them. Karen, right? Hi, hello, sorry to keep you waiting."

He stood up and moved around his desk to shake her hand. He was not quite six feet tall, slender, and he moved gracefully, like a ballroom dancer.

"Thank you for taking the time to see me," he said, "I really appreciate it. And I hope that what I'm about to propose could make it worth your while."

He's thanking me for my time. Jesus, she thought, how charming can this guy be?

"I understand that you are Elliot Spivaka's granddaughter? I know Elliott from some transactions I was involved with down in Fort Lauderdale. He's a great man, a real credit to his community. Well, let me be candid. He called and told me about your recent difficulty. I'm glad to see you looking so well, in fact."

She shrunk in her seat a bit when her "difficulty" came up, something she'd be living with forever, she supposed glumly.

"So, Elliot thought that you might do well to take some time off, think about things. Perhaps decide where you want your life to go, now that you're ready to start fresh.

"When he called, it occurred to both of us, damn near simultaneously, that you could do this while also doing another one of our friends a great service."

She wondered how much longer she'd have to sit here until he zeroed in on just what he wanted.

"Elliot's best friend is a man named Eben Whittaker, who lives in the Washington, D.C., area. He's older than your grandfather, he's eighty-six, and he owns land here out by Dulles Airport. Do you know where that is? No, I didn't think so. Eben lives in a cabin on his land, 1,375 acres in the middle of a very dynamic area with plenty of activity going on because of the airport. The entire region has been revitalized by the new commitment to develop the area. Eben is in position to complete the birth of a new city while also gaining a richly deserved financial reward by selling his land."

Caso rested on the arm of a chair next to Karen's. He turned his hands up in a gesture of supplication and said, "He won't sell."

He folded his hands and, perched above her, waited for her to respond.

"Why not?" she said, not sure she really wanted to be drawn into this story.

"Because he's eccentric and lonely. He lives alone, he has no family, and he says he wants to save the land for conservation. People have offered to retain part of the farm as parkland, but he says that's not enough. And now it's been reported that his health is failing."

He waited again, and she couldn't think of anything else to say except, "So?"

"Well, there's no will. The land could be divided equitably for development and parkland, but it could take years in probate. Yet, poor old Eben just sits out there, unhappy, waiting to die, unwilling to write a proper will."

"Excuse me, Mr. Caso—" she said.

"Bill. Please, call me Bill."

"Yeah, well, excuse me, but why am I hearing this?"

"Good question, excellent question," Caso said, raising a finger in approbation. "Because you can help Eben Whittaker while also helping yourself."

"I don't understand. What am I supposed to do?"

He stood up and walked back to his desk to perch there. "I've arranged through your grandfather for you to go out to Eben's place to stay for a time. Your grandfather asked Eben if you could stay with him until you had decided what you wanted to do next. Eben agreed."

"I see. And, then what?"

"Why, nothing," Caso said. "Take care of yourself. Enjoy the countryside. Decide what you want to do. And also, see how old Eben's doing. He's getting on, he'll be glad to have a bright, young woman such as yourself around to cheer the place up."

"Do you want me to spy on this old man, or try to influence him somehow?"

Caso closed his eyes and flattened his lips in mild disdain. "No, of course not. Don't even give it a passing thought. Much too Machiavellian to think about. I'm a practical man; if he tells you that he's thinking of selling, I'd like to know. But, please, do not do anything untoward. You understand, Eben won't even talk to developers at this juncture."

"I understand."

"Excellent! And listen, since you are doing this for me and for your grandfather as well as yourself, I think it only appropriate that you gain something from it to help you begin your future plans."

She said nothing as he said, "No, I insist," moving behind his desk. He scribbled, then tore out a check and handed it to her.

"Expenses. I'll keep an account going for you while you're at Eben's. And, have a wonderful time," he said, gesturing for her to rise. He ushered her out with one hand lightly touching her shoulder blade, "Relax. Have fun."

He walked her down the dusty hall to the elevator. "Look at this mess."

He glanced at her as they walked side by side, grinning, "I suppose you're wondering why I'm up here in an office building that's mostly bare steel? I made a bet that I'd be sitting in my office two years from project approval. The permits came so late that the only way I could win was to build my office first. Pretty silly, huh?" he said, taking on a sheepish look. "But I won the bet. Here's your elevator. Call me in a few weeks, tell me how you're doing."

After a warm handshake and smile, he was off, out of earshot as she called out from the closing doors, "How do I get there from here?"

On ground level, she walked to the street and looked for the cab. Gone, she thought, with my bags in the trunk. But squinting, she spotted it parked across the broad street, pulled around in the opposite direction. Beneath the basket two figures now jumped and ran after the ball.

She crossed the street and watched the cabdriver try to defend against a tall, attenuated Black man wearing long slacks, running shoes, and a worn printed shirt with a shapeless dull sweater over top. He shrugged his body, then flashed past the cabdriver to lay the ball in the basket.

"Take that, White boy."

"Mousey, you couldn't do that again in a million years."

The tall man set up again, feinted, and leaped for the basket. The cabdriver smacked the ball out of his hands before he could raise it to the hoop.

"Foul," the Black man barked.

"Foul?"

"That's right, nigger, you fouled me."

"Nigger, White boy, make up your mind, Mousey. Anyway, that's no foul, your hand's part of the ball."

"My hand? And my wrist and my elbow? Bullshit!"

As they both laughed, the cabdriver took the ball to the foul line. "Now, I'm going to show you some Sunday shit, boy."

"Who you calling boy?" the Black man said as he swatted the ball away from the basket.

The cabdriver giggled as he retrieved it, saying, "Jesus, Mousey, I'm going to have to get devious."

He lined up again, ready to move, when she called out, "Hey."

He relaxed and looked her way.

"Don't you want this fare?" she said.

He smirked, "Sure, lady, just as soon as I teach Mousey here some physics."

He dropped the ball, dribbled to his right and launched a wide hook shot up over the Black man's fully extended arms. As their bodies fell together in a heap on the macadam, the ball went high up on the backboard, touched it barely, and dropped through the naked hoop.

The two men fell over each other, laughing uproariously. After they gave each other high fives, low fives, and intermediate fives, the cabdriver strolled toward her, stooping to pick up his flannel shirt on the way.

"Let's go."

When they reached the car, an old Chevy sedan, she said, "You didn't especially wait for me, did you?"

He peeled off his drenched T-shirt and put on his flannel one, saying, "Truthfully, no. But here I am, and I do have your bags in the trunk. So, where are we going?"

"Fair Hills Farm, somewhere in Loudoun County."

He did a double take. "Loudoun County? Lady, we're in Washington, D.C. Do you know where Loudoun County is?"

"No," she said, unsure, "I'm from Florida."

He draped his wet shirt over the back seat of the cab. "You have any money?"

"I have this check," she said. She handed it to him, "We could go to a bank."

He whistled, "William Caso's personal check. Very impressive. But it's Sunday." He thought for a second, then said, "Oh well, climb in. You can pay me later."

Karen reached for the rear door, then stopped, looking at the soaked shirt covering the seat.

"Oh," he said, "Sorry. Mind riding up front?"

They passed Glebe Road on Route 66 before he asked her.

"So, what's William Caso giving you his personal check for, if I miht ask?"

Karen stared at him, half-smiling, half open-mouthed in amazement. "You might ask, but I might not answer."

"You might not."

She turned to the front, not really seeing the sound barriers or the other cars. "I got in trouble back home. Caso's a friend of my grandfather, so they hatched something together involving me."

"What kind of trouble were you in?"

"I had a little habit. I was teaching, and, uh, they fired me."

"I see. Are you clean now?"

"Five months and three days." She wondered why she was telling this cabdriver her life story, but she found it easy to do, too. He was a nice-enough looking guy, he seemed smart and he seemed to care a little in a sort of devil-may-care way. "I got into it because I was bored, I guess. Anyway, it's over. I'm not going back."

"Good."

When they got to Route 29, he said, "So, what does Caso want you to do with Eben Whittaker?"

She gazed at him again with surprise. "How did you know I was going to see Eben Whittaker?"

"He owns Fair Hills Farm. Shit, anyone who lives in D.C. and reads the paper knows who he is. Anyone who follows business, anyway. Real estate is important business in D.C. That, and selling government secrets."

"Oh. Whittaker is the so-called best friend of my grandfather. I'm supposed to be going out there for R and R. But I think they want me to find out if Whittaker has plans to sell the place. He's supposed to be sick."

"That's a hell of a retainer Caso gave you just to ask him a question everyone knows the answer to. But I didn't know he was sick."

"Well, he's supposed to be. I don't know. I guess I'll be finding out."

"Yeah."

When they started down the lane that five miles later would put them at Whittaker's cabin door, she asked him, "What's your name?"

"Bob Devenny."

"I'm Karen Spivaka."

"Slovak, huh? You don't look the part."

"Oh? What do I look like?"

"California beach chickie."

"I see. Well, you don't look like a cabdriver, either. You don't act like one."

"Right. I got rid of my grown-up job so I could play more ball. I didn't realize drivers work 16 hours a day."

"But you're still playing ball."

"Yeah, I got another job."

"Doing what?"

"Private dick."

"Get out," she laughed, "You're not serious?"

"Sure. I do a lot of divorce work. Stakeouts. No one notices a cab, or a cabbie asleep in the front seat."

"Jesus," she said, "that's a new one."

"Not really. Even so, don't be telling anyone, either. You'll blow my cover."

She shook her head, truly amused.

"Here we are."

They'd arrived at the front of a white clapboard farmhouse, its paint peeling in long strips. A large, black wooden barn, also badly in need of painting, stood to the right, and several smaller sheds leaned every which way in the rear of the house. She saw a rusted machine with curved blades sticking up between the barn and the house. Parked to the right was a dark green pickup truck with wooden sideboards. A huge crack ran the length of the truck's windshield like a river on a map, tributaries going off in different directions.

She took at the hills on either side of the buildings, barely hued a light green shade in the new spring weather, dotted by clumps of wild onions rushing the season. A twisted tree stood in front of the house, apple, she imagined, though without any apples growing, how could she know? For what she knew about horticulture it could be dogwood, she thought.

Devenny jumped out of the car and headed back to its trunk. A tiny old man appeared at the front door of the house, which rested on a concrete foundation. He had a full gray beard and wore a flannel shirt and jeans.

"You Karen Spivaka?"

"You're Mr. Whittaker?"

"Eben. I'm old, but not that old. Don't worry, I promise not to chase you around the kitchen table. Can you cook?"

"Not too well."

"I'm a terrific cook. Well, c'mon, kiddo, get your gear up here."

Devenny clean and jerked one of two Samsonite bags onto the porch. "Hello, old timer," he said as he hoisted up the second.

"You been watching too many Westerns, son. That's Mr. Old Timer to you."

Devenny grinned and said, "Yeah, well, I don't intend to be here that long—unless you want to sell me your farm, say, for a dollar. You know, a sudden attack of Oldtimer's Disease?"

Whittaker guffawed broadly, hands on his knees.

"No go, huh? I didn't think so."

"You are a smart-ass, aren't you."

"The only saving grace of hack jockeys."

"Say, where did you get that shirt?" the old man said.

"Army-Navy in Wheaton."

"Huh. Looks good. I always get L.L. Bean."

"That's fine if you want to pay for the designer look," Devenny said as he followed the old man in with the bags. The old man laughed, "Smart-ass."

Bewildered, but also hopeful, Karen trailed behind.

"So, how have you been, Karen?"

Caso wore a pale gray suit, also double-breasted, of a feather-light fabric that complemented the last of the spring weather verging upon summer wetness. They sat at a table for lunch in an open-air café on 19th Street NW. A quilt of fresh green leaves on the surrounding trees partially blocked the sun, allowing patches of light to dapple the tablecloth.

He sipped slowly from mineral water garnished with lime as he waited for her reply.

"I've been well. It's been a good time for me, just as you said it would be."

"Excellent. I'm glad that's true. And how is Eben?"

"Fantastic. He's amazing for his age, a real character. I guess it's been okay for him, too, because he's fine, no signs of poor health or anything. We do a lot of hiking, picnics, and gardening. Devenny even brought some bicycles out one time, so that we could—"

"Devenny? Who's Devenny?"

"Well, he's a taxi driver who first took me out to the farm. I've sort of been seeing him since I arrived."

"Oh, that's nice. A taxi driver, huh? Are you getting serious about him?"

She shrugged, "I don't know. I don't see that much of him, he drives in the city. Unless he gets a fare to Dulles, I just see him on weekends. He's not himself a very serious guy, I think. But he's nice." Then, beginning to laugh, she said, "He's funny, too. We'll be driving in town for dinner or something and if he sees a fare, he'll pick him up."

Caso joined in her laughter, "Well, a man has to make a living."

"I guess so," she agreed.

"He has to be able to afford the best for you."

"Sure."

Caso twirled his glass by the stem, gazing at the slice of lime as it drifted and spun with the movement of the water. "Karen," he said, "you mentiond that Eben is well. I suppose he's doing what he's always done?"

Here it comes, she thought, the meeting part of the meeting. "I guess so. He gardens and walks around a lot. And he talks. All the time. He loves to talk about the old days, or sometimes yelling about county crooks or how crooked developers are."

She put her hand up to cover her mouth. "Oops. Sorry."

He waved it off. "He hasn't said anything about the future, I take it."

"Nothing about his land, if that's what you mean."

"That's exactly what I mean. Have you asked him about what he has in mind for it?"

"No. How can I do that? I'm his guest. How can I ask him what happens after he dies?"

Caso stopped spinning the glass. He folded his hands on the table. "Karen, events have occurred recently that make it opportune to determine Eben's intentions regarding Fair Hills Farm. I'm not at liberty to explain fully, but I can say that if certain interests could learn Eben's plans for the disposition of the place, if we could learn that imminently, it could lead to a very positive situation."

"Mr. Caso," she said, "I know you sent me out there to find that out—come on, really. But I can't just ask him, 'Is there a will, are you going to sell your land?' How is that going to sound after he's put me up?"

"Karen," Caso said, reaching over to place his hand upon hers, "I don't want to involve you in all of the details regarding the potential here. But I have to tell you that a great deal of money is at stake. And one of those with a major interest in learning what I'm asking you is your grandfather."

"My grandfather?" An unsettling ripple coursed through her stomach. She sat quietly, darting her eyes back and forth from the tabletop to Caso. "What would my grandfather have to do with a real estate deal all the way up here?"

Caso sat back. Solemnly, he said, "Let me just say that his interests range far. Also, allow me to tell you something I'm sure he never would. That is, he's made extensive investments in the Washington area and many of them have yielded disappointing results, very disappointing. I won't say more except that your grandfather has much at stake in the information that we're discussing."

Caso sat back and sipped his water, waiting silently. Karen's entire body seemed to deflate.

"What do you want me to do?"

"So, why so sad, Sweetie?" Devenny said, angling his way into traffic.

"Caso is really pressuring me to find out what Eben's plans are. Now, he says my grandfather has a lot of money at stake."

"Huh. That's weird. Eben's been sitting on that land for years. Why such a big deal now?"

"I don't know. Caso wouldn't say."

"Something must be up. I wonder what Caso knows that we don't. Or Eben. Here we are."

He parked the cab under the Whitehurst Freeway and led the way up to Wisconsin Avenue. "Ah, my favorite Georgetown establishment, Mr. Smith's."

"Why so?"

"Because it's the nighttime mecca of entertainment in Washington, the toniest part of town, where it is, you know, 'at' — okay, it's cheap."

"You take me to all the best places," she breathed, leaning into him, batting her lashes.

"Who loves you, baby?"

They were halfway through their sandwiches and beers when a bottle of champagne arrived at their table.

"Gosh, Devenny, I am impressed. What is this, the anniversary of our first month together?"

"You know me better than that. I didn't order this." He looked at the waitress and she said, "Over there, the two suits."

They turned to look at two immaculately appointed men, almost mirror images of each other in Italian suits and shoes topped off by precise haircuts, not too long, not too short. One of them was in his early forties, the other seemed to be about twenty-five, though he sported a moustache, perhaps to affect wiser years. Seeing them sitting at a garden table covered by a red and white checkered plastic, tablecloth amid the fronds of an artificial tree, Karen almost laughed at how out of place they seemed to be.

"Who are they?" she asked.

"I don't know, but from their spiffy duds, I'd say they usually dine down the street. My guess is that they run with the same pack as Caso."

Karen and Devenny finished their meal, every now and then slipping a gander over at the other table. On one of their glances, they caught the two men standing up and buttoning their double-breasted jackets in unison. Then they started walking to the couple's table.

"I hope you don't mind the intrusion," the older one said as he reached out his hand. "I'm Sandy Adams. This is my associate, David Snyder. You mind?" he said, drawing up a chair.

He had sandy hair she noted, and reddish skin. He wore a gold watch and two gold rings, one a wedding ring. The younger man wore a wedding ring, too, gold with a small circle of diamonds around the edge. His complexion was peaches and cream and his hair was very dark, black, matching the black opal of his eyes.

"Thanks for the bubbly," Devenny said. "Why'd you send it?"

"A congratulatory gesture," Adams said. "Correct me if I'm wrong, you are Karen Spivaka, are you not?"

"Yes," she said, slightly puzzled.

"How do you know her?" Devenny said.

"This is a small town, Mr. Devenny. People doing deals make it even smaller." He turned to Karen, "You're staying with Eben Whittaker, am I correct?"

Karen didn't answer, instead glancing at Devenny. He raised his eyes and shrugged, turning his hands up in a "what can you do" gesture.

"Yes," she said.

"Unhuh. Very interesting. I don't suppose you're representing yourself?" When she didn't reply, he said, "Look, everyone's interested in what the old man will do with the land. So, when a new player comes in from—excuse me," he reached over and pressed a thumb lightly on her arm, observing the color as it returned, "from Florida, I'd say. I'd say that's a Florida tan, wouldn't you, Davey? Mine's Cancun. Anyway, you're new in town and you're hobnobbing with one of the most eligible land lovers in the area. Inquiring minds want to know—namely myself and Davey here for starters—if there's any movement going on out there."

Karen frowned, then said, "Why should I tell you anything? I don't even know you."

"I know," he said. "This is really very impolite of me, barging in on your dinner like this. Please forgive me, it's just so fascinating when something new pops up." He produced a card from his jacket pocket. "I'm a partner at Harris, Colbor, and Lee, one of the major, full-service real estate companies in the Metro area. So, obviously, it goes without saying that if Eben Whittaker is ready to negotiate for his land, we'd like to make an offer."

Devenny shook his head, "Geez, first Caso, now you."

Karen shot him a look that could kill.

"Caso?" Adams said. "Is that who you've been talking to? Listen, never let it be said that I would bad mouth a great developer like William Caso. He's had great vision in the past, but—I shouldn't be speaking out of school—he's overextended. His ability to raise capital now is in question. His plans for the Fourth Street project are in serious jeopardy. The District government won't give him anymore permits without housing concessions, and he can't do that and arrive at the proper margin. His vision was great, he envisioned another Rock Center or his own Trump Tower. But, frankly, instead of that, he's coming up with a Chump Tower. Believe me. If Eben Whittker is ready to sell, we're ready to deal. It's been a pleasure meeting you."

He stood up, smiled beatifically, shook their hands and left, closely followed by the other well-dressed man.

"Well," Devenny said, "what do you think of that? The plot thickens."

"Why did you tell him about Caso?" Karen snapped.

"Hey, lighten up, I didn't think it was a state secret. Besides, this is Washington. Do you really think he didn't know what was what before we sat down? I wanted to see his reaction. He slammed Caso pretty good, I'd say. Now I'm really curious about all the sudden interest in Eben's farm."

She didn't say anything, twisting the corner of her napkin.

He drove them up to Adams Morgan where they danced to the Reggae music at Kilimanjaro's, sometimes languidly, sometimes hot. Seeing him pose outrageously, then flash his winning boyish smile, she felt her heart skip, only to falter with doubt about his seriousness, his stamina, his staying power. Such thoughts made her see how she had changed almost into an adult, she realized, smiling sadly, sweetly.

At midnight, they wearily climbed back into the cab. He turned the corner at California and a figure waved at them, a blur running to open the rear door and jump in.

"Sorry, buddy, I'm not in service."

"Never mind, Devenny, drive downtown. I won't be with you long."

Together, Karen and Devenny peered around to see who it was behind them. David Snyder sat in the middle of the back seat, wiping his nose with a handkerchief.

"Uh, the pollen in this town, it kills me. Go on, drive down Eighteenth Street. I'll get out there."

Karen watched Devenny grimace as he put the car in gear. Keeping his eyes on the road, he said, "So, where's your boss, Snyder?"

"Hearth side. He's a good man, a family man. The sentiment 'brokers are whores' doesn't apply to him."

"Oh?"

"Yeah. Not that he won't get done what needs to be done, mind you. When matters are at stake, important things, well, sometimes they call for drastic action."

"I don't believe I'm following you, Davey."

"I'm not talking to you, Devenny."

Karen glanced back to find Snyder leaning forward near her side of the seat. She noted the breadth of his pupils, dilated in the night.

"This Eben Whittaker affair, Ms. Spivaka, could be very important, quite critical. It could get very dicey. A lot is at stake and not just for Caso. If money won't do it, well," he dipped his head as though acknowledging the plain truth, "other things might."

"Hey!" she cried in a small voice.

Devenny jerked the car to the curb. "Snyder, what the fuck do you think you're saying?"

"Nothing, nothing. No one's desperate, here. Never mind, Devenny. It's all right, this is my stop."

He opened the door and stepped halfway out of the cab. He turned in her direction again, "Just remember, if you really want to work a deal that will get the most out of it for you, forget Caso. Forget Adams. I'm not tied up. I'm the player you might need."

"A real player," Devenny said.

"That's right. Give me a call, Ms. Spivaka, if I can help you with Mr. Whittaker."

He walked off, disappearing through the door of a club, allowing a brief blast of steel music to escape into the night as he entered.

"Karen, what the hell was that all about?"

"How should I know? I don't know what he was talking about."

"I think we have to talk to the old man."

When they awakened Eben and told him, before he allowed them to continue, he stepped around the farmhouse in silence, turning up the kerosene lamps to bring the large common room to life with warm light. She'd enjoyed his deliberate quaintness, the fact that even though he had electricity, he refused to use it on a day-to-day basis. "How do you think I got rich, by using electricity like an ass? Too expensive," he'd said. "I just keep it in case of emergency. Also, keeps the place's value up."

He had a phone, too, out in the toolshed in the back. Once a day he would trudge out to call his lawyer, his accountant, his various consultants and partners. "Money means work. You've got to keep on top of it or it goes away," he'd say.

She found his stubborn clinging to the trappings of rustic living charming. The dried rushes hanging from the walls next to cast iron skillets, pots, and pans, the oak tables and chairs, the wood-burning stove, the giant blue glass jars filled with oats, rice, beans, tea, and a mix of grains struck her as something out of a children's book, or a Shaker dream. Eben had no rugs, just hardwood floors immaculately clean. He enjoyed his rocker next to the stove, reading while listening to music from his stereo, his only concession to electricity. Though his existence was one utterly foreign to her, she'd learned to relish it. Perhaps she enjoyed it because it was totally different from her own life, she mused. Now, it might be threatened.

He sat in his rocker, not speaking, thinking. He said, "Caso said there were reports that I was sick?"

"Yes," she said quietly.

"And he mentioned there was no will?"

"Yes. He said that the land would forever be tied up in court if you died without a will."

"Heh. I don't think that's so. The county will move things along, don't you worry. They see my land as a potential tax base, believe me." He thought more, rubbing his beard with his hand, mumbling, "I wonder how he found out about that stuff, though. Must have made some donations to local medical practices."

Karen and Devenny shot each other stark looks. "Is any of it true, Eben?" asked Devenny.

"Well, as a matter of fact, yes. There is no will for Eben Whittaker," he smiled slightly, "and I do have cancer, a lower-end kind. It's under control somewhat, as much as the bright, young physicians can manage, anyway. And, when you get old, cancer takes its time killing you. Hell, I'll probably die of something else, some other old age ailment. But, Caso knows about this. He's pressuring you, Karen, about a will or selling. And that little prick working for Adams threatened you, all because there's no will. That's not good," he laughed cheerlessly.

"Eben," Devenny said, "do you have a lawyer you trust?"

"Sure. Or, I should say had. He's been dead fifteen years. But his kid's in the firm and he minds my paperwork. He'll do."

"Well, then, why don't you have him write a will? Leave it to some nature foundation or something if you want. Then, everyone's off the hook."

"Now, that's no solution. See what happened to Claude Moore and his bequest? They sold it! The only thing that kept it intact that long was the old fart refused to die. I can't count on living as long as old Claude, either. No, it'll have to be something else."

He rubbed his chin again. "Okay," he said at length. "I think I know what I need to know. Good night, kids."

He pulled himself up from the chair and slowly ascended the stairs to bed.

Karen watched him. Then, with eyes brimming she said, "Devenny!"

He embraced her, hugging her close.

"It's okay. He'll be all right. But I think I better do some research on Caso, see if I can find out what he's up to."

"And how do you expect to do that?" she asked.

"You forget. I'm a gumshoe. I have my sources."

Eben hardly talked to her the next morning, or for the next few days. He spent an inordinate amount of time in the toolshed on the phone. At the end of the week, he trudged back from the shed and said to her, "Karen, I want you to go into town. I want you to stay there for the day. Go shopping. Here's some money. Don't come back until evening."

She met Devenny at the Tune Inn, and he looked grim. "This is what I found out. You remember Mousey, the guy I was playing ball with when you first met Caso? Right, well his girlfriend works for First American Bank. She's a trainee for management. So, Rita knows other managers that were trainees like her from around town, you know, members of the sisterhood. They'd meet at seminars, stuff like that. I told Mousey about our problems and he got Rita to talk to a friend of hers who is now a manager at National Federal." He nodded when Karen opened her mouth about to speak. "Right. Caso's bank for the new building. Rita's friend nosed around. Caso is personally on the snide for eighty-five million dollars of that mixed-use project on Fourth Street, the one you visited. And a big interest payment is coming due, and he's stretched over another project out in Loudoun County."

"What does that mean?" she said.

"It means his credit stinks, and he has to cough up four mil in two weeks."

"Oh."

"'Oh' is right, Karen. But he could get well, credit-wise, if investors knew he had an option on Eben's land. He could cut a deal in which they would pay off his note on his little Fourth Street problem as part of their dues for getting in on Fair Hills Farm."

"I see. But why did he bring me into all this? What am I doing in this mess?"

Devenny hesitated, then said, "Karen, your grandad is a partner in the Fourth Street project. He's out ten million himself. Since he's Eben's best friend, you're the leverage."

"I can't believe anything I can do would work with Eben."

Devenny shrugged. "That's not all. The third partner on the deal is Sandy Adams."

"Sandy Adams? But he was down on Caso so much."

"Adams is out twenty million, too. Maybe he's a little pissed."

"Yeah, maybe."

"Anyway, it's getting late. Let's go see what Eben has up his sleeve."

When they arrived, they found Eben at the table, his hands folded in front of him, nursing a mug of tea. He smiled wickedly and said, "I think I've got this little matter sorted out."

Before he could finish, Devenny filled him in on what he'd learned from Mousey's girlfriend. The smile faded from the old man's face as he listened to the details.

"So, Karen, your old grandad has himself in a fix." He pinched his lips together, swinging his head in rueful judgement. "Looks like I don't have everything figured out after all."

He rose abruptly and worked his way to the screen door, which slammed shut hard behind him.

Karen and Devenny exchanged glances. "Where do you think he's going?"

Devenny slid over to the door and peered out. "To the shed." He looked back to Karen, "He's making another call."

The old man didn't return for more than an hour. Karen and Devenny pulled up chairs, she at the table, he in the old man's rocker near the stove, one leg draped over an arm. They waited.

She wondered what Eben was doing. Who he was talking to? She wondered what Devenny thought about it or about anything. He was a smart guy, she'd learned. So, could he really only be interested in basketball or just the fun of the moment?

And, what about me? she thought. What am I doing here? She admitted that she had no particular desire to be anywhere else, and as she whiled away the time, Caso kept plunking money into her account.

He's said there'd be more, too, a lot more if Eben sold. But she liked Eben, he treated her really well. What was she going to do, though, if he died? She'd never be able to teach again, not that she cared. But she'd need money. She sighed angrily.

"Well," said Eben when he came back in, "let's go to bed. Busy day, tomorrow." He ambled up the stairs.

Devenny stared at Karen. She twisted her head in the direction of the old man's disappearance and said, "Well, goddamn."

Devenny dropped her off in front of the entrance to Caso's new building, now bearing a sign proclaiming it 1000 Fourth Street. Since her first visit a month ago the steel frame had been completely enclosed in polished stone, though construction continued on the interior. As she walked through the new brass and glass doors, past the newly installed marble facades in the lobby, she acted as though she didn't hear the whistles and propositions from the hard hats on the way. On the thirteenth floor, the doors opened to reveal the same splendid hall, immaculately clean this time. Office workers passed back and forth as she made her way to the double brass doors of Caso's office. Before she reached them, she ducked into a women's room.

The old man had been mysteriously secretive that morning, refusing to answer her questions. And, when he'd taken Devenny out to the yard for a private conversation, she'd really been furious. Then, he'd given her the envelope for Caso.

He hadn't said not to look inside, but it was taped shut. Taped, not sealed. The envelope was of a heavy cotton weave with a brace of names on the upper right-hand corner declaring it from some law firm. She knew she shouldn't open it, but this was as much about her as Eben Whittaker. And why was she the only one who didn't know anything? Screw it, she said to herself, using one fingernail to pry the tape carefully apart from the edge of the envelope.

"Being of sound mind and . . ." It was a will, an enormous sheaf of papers stapled together. She paged to the back and found Eben's signature, dated yesterday. While she'd been shopping, of course. She took the papers into a stall, locked the door, sat down, and slowly began to read through the document.

"Did you look inside this?" Caso asked her, holding up the will in one hand, the envelope in the other by his side..

"Yes," she said.

He gazed at her for a moment, his face empty of expression. He turned his attention to the will and began to scan as he said, "Did you read it?"

"Of course."

"He's named you the executrix. But that's it, that's all. You receive nothing."

"I know. But you got what you wanted. He's left you the land. So, what do you do now, kill him?"

He stared at her, startled. "What are you talking about? Why would you say such an outlandish thing? What's wrong with you?"

"What's wrong with me? What did you do to make him leave you the land? I can't believe he's doing it just because my grandfather's losing money on your project. Old Grandpop's got plenty of money, believe me."

Again, Caso seemed surprised. His face hardened, "So, you know about that. Who told you? Eben? Your grandfather, perhaps. Or, perhaps it was Sandy Adams. Yes, I know you talked to him. What, do you think, I'm foolish? I've kept track of you and your cabdriver Lothario."

"Unhuh," she said, her face flushing red, "never mind me, what about Eben?"

"Eben? He's dying. Six months tops, according to his physicians. The land will go to someone else one way or another, so it's going to me. I've made sure of that. Oh, not just to take care of this place." He rolled his eyes to the ceiling, "The potential of Fair Hills Farm is unbelievable. Right smack in the middle of Loudoun County, minutes from Dulles, on top of the toll road. Amazing!" he said in a buoyant, reverent tone.

"Anyway, don't be so dramatic. The length of Eben's life isn't the leverage, this is," he said, waving the will as he headed to his desk. As he picked up the receiver, waiting for the autodial to complete cycling the numbers, he said, "Thank you, Karen. You did well. You won't be forgotten."

She stepped over to his desk and said loudly, "Why are you doing this? Why do you need more?"

He lowered the receiver and said, "I create places to work, and homes. Where are the hundreds of thousands of people projected to come into this area in the next two decades supposed to live and work? Or, don't you want them to move here? You, a month off a plane from Florida." He screwed up his mouth in a disdainful smirk, "Don't start proselytizing now, Karen. You did agree to stay with Eben. Was it for the money I put aside for you or did you fear being cut out of Grandpop's will? After all, you did say he had plenty of money, didn't you?"

"You bastard, I'm already out of his will. Don't you know he's a leader in the war against drugs?"

He nodded, "Of course. How else could you ingratiate your way back into the fold? You impress me, Karen. I'll be sure that you receive the credit that you deserve."

She refused to say a word to Devenny on the way back to the farm. Devenny sang and joked, but she would have none of it. The bastard wouldn't tell her about his doings with Eben, so screw him.

They reached the lane in full darkness. Devenny slowed down to avoid the hidden ruts and potholes. They crested the final rise and began to roll down toward the loop in front of the house. The windows glowed dimly from the kerosene lamps, and they could just make out the soft airs of a violin playing a classical melody.

They were near the trees when she saw the strange black shape in front of the steps, a car.

"Whose ride is that?" Devenny asked, stopping the cab. Cobalt-blue light flashed in every window as a sharp report cracked the quiet night.

They froze, staring at the front of the house, dim again in the soft lamplight, again only hearing the faint strains of the stereo. In fluid motion, Devenny flicked the headlights and engine off, allowing the cab to drift down to the side of the house. He hissed, "Get down!"

They huddled low in the car, watching as the screen door snapped open, held by one arm. A figure followed, a man in a light blue suit with black hair and a moustache. He held a handgun low at his thigh. He appeared dazed, sweating. Without a glance one way or the other, he jumped from the porch to his car. He tore off into the night, leaping and bounding over the ruts in the lane.

"My God!" cried Karen, holding her fist to her mouth.

"Wait here," Devenny whispered.

"No!"

"Look," he rasped harshly, "Snyder is gone, we saw him leave. And I don't think you want to see the old man like this."

Without answering, she followed him closely into the house. In the kitchen on the floor next to the stove, she saw the old man crumpled on his side. She turned her head, sickened pale.

Devenny mumbled dully, "Eben's dead. Shot dead."

Karen keened a soft wail.

In the car, grasping the steering wheel hard, Devenny dipped his head. "Yeah. Fuck. Let's get out of here."

In a matter of hours, the police reeled David Snyder in somewhere in North Carolina, though the trial could be years off, they told her. She hadn't been surprised at how few people showed up at Eben's funereal out at the farm. Her grandfather's appearance did surprise her.

He at least seemed moved, she thought.

For herself, she'd been miserable, almost inconsolable. Devenny spent a lot of time with her trying to cheer her up. But he was sad, too.

She stayed out at Fair Hills Farm, straightening up, tending the garden, thinking about what she was going to do, until Caso's office called requesting a meeting. She was ready to tell him to kiss off, but Devenny convinced her to go.

When they entered the office, Caso sat behind his desk, and next to him on a divan sat Sandy Adams. A third man occupied a chair on the opposite side.

Caso did not get up. "Thank you for coming, Karen, Mr. Devenny. I believe you know Sandy Adams. This is Michael Gleason, Eben's attorney. I wanted to meet to discuss his will, to make sure that it is acquitted with the greatest expediency and without fuss. Since you are the executrix, I thought it only proper that we hold a preliminary meeting to assure that matters go smoothly."

She looked at him incredulously. "You can't be serious? You killed him! You or your partner there," she said, sneering at Adams.

"Now, Ms. Spivaka," Adams said, his hands upraised, "please don't start this way. I had no idea that Snyder was a cocaine addict or that he was in that kind of debt. He was one of my top brokers, like a son to me. If he'd come to me instead of trying to coerce poor old Eben, none of this would have happened."

"I'm so sure," she said, sullenly.

"Karen," Adams said, "David Snyder did a terrible thing. And what's more, why? What would anyone have to gain from murdering poor old Eben? It was horribly wrong and it was senseless. If you'll forgive me for sounding so insensitive, I do it only to make it obvious that we wouldn't be involved in this even if we could be so base, it's senseless from a business point of view. No one wants to be in court for years trying to resolve issues raised by violent acts."

"That's correct," Caso said. "I'd like to do this with Mr. Gleason's and your help to make this as painless as possible."

"Sure," said Devenny quietly, "but what about Eben's other wills?"

No one said a word, all suddenly staring at Devenny. He sat on the edge of his seat, knees apart, hands casually clasped between them. Karen gazed at him incongruously noting how nice he looked in his suit and without the cap. His cowlick in front was still out of control though.

"What are you talking about?" Caso said coolly.

"The wills Eben sent off to the Nature Conservancy, Loudoun County, the U.S. Department of the Interior, and the State of Virginia, leaving Fair Hills Farm to each of them. Oh, and he gave me these to pass out, too."

Devenny stood up and reached into the breast pocket of his jacket to extract several envelopes. "One for you," he said, handing an envelope to Adams, "one for you," he said to Karen, "one for me, of course," he said and as he turned to Caso, "and you already have yours."

Devenny sat back down. "Each one drawn up by a different law firm in town, excluding your firm, Mr. Gleason. He didn't want to compromise you. Each one signed on the same day. It took some real driving to get old Eben around town to sign them all. Good thing he knew an experienced cabdriver. Anyway, each will leaves the farm to the person who just received it, respectively. The other ones are in the mail."

"You don't expect me to take this seriously?" Caso said.

"Oh, yeah." Devenny glanced at his wristwatch, "And if you hurry, you can beat the rush to apply for probate for yours. Maybe that'll count for something in court."

"Why, you idiot! Do you know what you're fucking up here?" Adams shouted, half-rising to his feet, his tan face vividly crimson now.

"Hey, buddy, you know how it is," Devenny said, "when something needs to get done, it gets done."

Adams blinked, his eyes narrowing. Caso stopped him before he could speak.

"Relax, Sandy. I've already secured refinancing for 1000 Fourth Street. Business will go on as usual. But I have to hand it to old Eben. A cute trick, a play that Shakespeare would have loved, as the young Turks like to say. Of course, all the wills will be no good, which means that the land will end up belonging to the state after all. So, the price goes up. But I'll own it, no matter what. Thank you very much, Mr. Devenny."

"You're welcome, Mr. Caso. And Mr. Adams, if I were you I'd still try for probate. Who knows if Mr. Caso is entirely correct or objective in his assessment of the situation? Am I right in this, Mr. Gleason?"

"The law is strange," the third man said, a graying thin figure in a gray herringbone suit.

Karen and Devenny were waiting at the elevator door when Gleason caught up with them. As they stepped into the car, he said, "Ms. Spivaka, I have this to give to you."

He handed her an envelope. Inside, she found a yellowing document with two new pages attached at the end.

Gleason left them on the broad sidewalk in front of the building, with Karen reading the will. It was the same as the others, except for the codicil on the first new page stating that Fair Hills Farm was to be left in a trust, of which she was the guardian. She turned to the last page.

"Devenny, this will is signed Charles Spivaka!"

He nodded solemnly, "Yeah, this is the one you'll want to keep. Eben's real name was Charles Spivaka. He was your grandfather's brother, your great uncle. He started using the name Eben Whittaker back in the day to avoid the draft. That was the leverage your grandfather had on him. But Eben really didn't care anymore. What were they going to do, put him in jail? Anyway, when push comes to shove, this will should keep the dogs at bay, the land intact. He never did change his name legally and the will was recorded back in the seventies, though the codicil was added by Gleason more recently. As Eben's attorney, Gleason was obligated to keep his mouth shut about this according to his client's final instructions. Though, with the likes of Caso and Adams at the door, I don't think it was hard for him to adhere to attorney-client privilege. Anyway, you're in line to inherit all that's left—though he did have to bail your granddad Elliot out to keep him quiet on this."

"Why didn't he tell me?" she said.

"Come on, Karen. You're your grandfather's daughter for God's sake. You were talking to Caso on a regular basis. How could he trust you if his own brother was turning the screws on him?"

"Well, why did he trust you?" she said, almost in a whine.

Devenny lifted his shoulders, "He knew I only wanted to play ball and get a new cab."

"I see," she said, thumbing through the bundled will. "I wonder what made him decide he could trust me now."

A thin piece of paper dropped from between the pages she held to the sidewalk. She picked it up.

"Ten million dollars."

"Jesus Christ! Let me see that." Devenny gazed at the check, whistling, "Will you look at that? Good God, also signed by Charles Spivaka." He glanced at her, "Old Eben just won your trust."

She took the check back, read it, and reread it.

"So, what are you going to do now?" Devenny asked.

"I don't know."

She caught the next plane to L.A.

Ghosting

Wayne saw a ghost and knew that his life was over, all the premises gone with the pretenses. He had to wonder who the ghost was. Was it his dead mother, his father, his brother long gone, or his sister dead from suffocating on the pill given to help her sleep? Was it the little boy with a stocking cap over his bald head, met in the third grade on the playground, and later in church imagined in his coffin? Was it a seeable ghost, a touchable ghost? Was it a ghost just out of sight in the corner of his eye or in his blind spot no matter which way his head turned? Was it a ghost of hope or one of horror? He had all of these questions to ask even as he felt the ghost enveloping him. He had to wonder if it would take shape, firm up, and change his life. Or did it mean the end of his life, period?

Analysis would free him of this ghost or not; he needed to discover if the magical lands brought to him by this ghost were the realms introduced by all spirits to wonderers, the excitement and need for apparitions of all other people save himself. Would towers, spires, emeralds, spatial curves, beautiful creatures, wings above visit him in the wake of the banshee of his mind? Would he be warned to kill his mother andhis father before they killed him, then kill himself? Was it simple madness?

God, a ghost. Flying in the high stratosphere airless, now in the dark of the sky, pinpointed by the lights of other minds or places, trying to break into the eternal night of his thoughts, maybe?

Perhaps he was simply sick. Sickness would cure him of this vision, or maybe he could walk out of this room and never have to face the fact that a ghost had filled his sight. Why are ghosts taller, he had to ask, or did they vary among those who saw them? Could he talk to the ghost?

Why come now? Wayne whined in his mind, too frightened by the possibilities to speak out loud, then petrified by the thought that the ghost could hear him anyway. Why didn't he run, run out the door, out of the room, away from the memory? Or, he could die from fright and escape his dread that way? Unless the ghost followed him into death after death and beyond, truly haunting him?

The thought haunted him. Did this go past hell, this persistent specter, did its existence change the ideas of life and death, or more importantly, the very shape of life and death? Hell, Heaven, and Earth were gone, dismissed by another unreal reality, could this be? If this was true, then was it a hell for him if it opposed what his life always had been, one of reining in the tension between emotion and rationality? How had this ghost come about?

He grabbed his head with his hands and kneaded his eyes free of the refracted presence of the apparition only to see phosphines of its image in the darkness left behind.

What is happening to me, he cried out silently.

He clenched his hands away from his eyes and tried to squeeze the brutal wraith from his mind—think, think!

Ghosts mean death. But who had died? Not me, Wayne thought, alive, thinking, as far as he knew. Unless, with the ghost came an existence separate from living.

Nothing had changed around him or in his mind. He could see the beat-up old desk where he had pounded out a living selling dream houses, fantasies of what life could be for others.

He held up his hands. His body hadn't changed, he could see every nail, count every sparse hair on his knuckles. He grabbed the picture of his ex-wife Ellen and his son Patrick, two years older now than in the photo. Twelve years since their separation, ten since the divorce, and he hadn't seen Patrick very much since.

Remembering the pain proved his past and he anticipated a future of some kind—the weekend, anyway.

A thought fled through his mind, voiced by a friend for whom he didn't have much respect. She once said to him how the real was never real, that the very substance of this little cabinet—she pounded it with her fist—wasn't solid or still, but moving all the time, molecules crashing against molecules, an amazing concept.

He'd been amazed that she was capable of even entertaining such an amazing concept. Oh, he knew it was true, but he never believed in his soul that he was a mess of moving particles, unsure of where they were, where they were going, or going to be. There had been bound-aries before the ghost.

On a day, strolling on a Fiji beach, past the fecund, rotting after-math of a typhoon, he passed by faded beige fronds at the feet of the stripped palms already greening again. Bleached nautilus shells lined up half buried next to others immersed in sea water. The gently moving waves framed the glory of the shells' decorative murals, red and brown Far East pavilions against a background fading pink to egg white. He was stopped by two Fijian kids, who introduced themselves and shook his hand very formally.

"If you buy a chicken," they said in sweet, sing-song English, "we will bring all the rest, the tapiocas, everything else, and have a cookout tomorrow."

He had to laugh, they were so straightforward about the deal, so guileless. He almost felt bad about prevaricating, somewhat guilty that he couldn't quite match their sweet honesty a hundred years removed from eating Captain Cook.

The shade hovered like milk sliding down the side of a glass and Wayne clutched groping for a hold.

He had seen the world in front of him and wondered what the hell was going on? He was troubled by the violence, the craziness, and he wondered. The things he knew to be true didn't jibe with the way he felt. He would watch TV and see crime, and he would see Black guys being hustled off for committing one horrific act after another, rape, muggings, killings, young, old, all running together. And he had to ask himself, dreading, why always Blacks?

Grab a cab in this town, and if the driver is from Ethiopia or some other African country, he's polite and friendly, glad to be here, glad to have the work. The encounter was a held breath releasing relief from the fearful image of the brooding local hip-hop gangsta and his attitude about popping you for the sins your grandfather committed. Get cut off by a taxi when driving your own car, though, and it didn't matter that you were never, ever to use that word, taught by parents long dead turned to dust—as soon as the cabby was seen as Black, the invective kept secretly in the soul would creep up, nigger. Adult usage.

Cold fingers melted into tendrils leaking around his mind, freezing his thoughts in horror of a known stranger.

"How do you feel about gays?" the boss's son had asked him, standing in line at an ivy-webbed school, a new university by popular state decree in Pennsylvania. The film society was showing "O Lucky Man," and they chatted spiritedly on the way to the film and waiting for tickets. The boss's son was tall, big nosed, curly-haired in a natural perm, sallow skinned, gentle and Jewish, he thought, enthusiastic about film and theater. In answer to his question, he vacillated, as though not much interested in the question.

Is he gay? He's so gay, he's ecstatic! his brother used to say, putting off anyone who might ask the question. Gay. How could they put their peters in a place like that? Fudge-packing, shock jocks mocked. And, he had done it, a couple of times, but with women. He'd come out touched by brown, but not like he'd thought.

He remembered as a kid the doctor's family next door, their beautiful, laughing baby boy, their youngest, who was retarded, it was learned. An inkling came from finding him picking through his diaper and eating his own shit.

The Chinese turn theirs into fertilizer, night soil, and raise their own food using it. That's what you have to do when you have a billion and a quarter people, eat shit or die. You can go to China, he thought, and see them take a live monkey and put him in the middle of a table with a special hole in it, so only the monkey's head clears the top. Then, they open up the top of his skull and eat his brains while he squirms and squeals until all of his thoughts and actions have been gobbled up. Or was that just another apocryphon from *Mondo Cane*?

Jews love Chinese food.

The boss's son was a Jew. Not handsome, pleasant. Wayne had chased the boss's son's sister after that, sexy in barely a bikini at the company picnic. They'd gone to the movies, too.

"So, what'd you think?" he'd asked her.

"I liked it," she'd said, "there were a lot of interesting things to see."

He did an internal double-take, then reminding himself that she was an art student, a different way of looking at life as things to see. He'd run into her again at a party at her brother's row house, a grand Victorian affair in the middle of town. Passing by the upstairs hall, he glanced at a couple and saw the brother kissing a slight, blond youth. Deeply, passionately.

He'd been stunned. Like the girl he'd dated down the block whom he'd see once a month to take to a movie, then to her home to screw. He'd met her in the local watering hole in the same jerkwater small Pennsylvania town with its stupid molecules bouncing around. Small town life, and she'd been so taken by his chatter patter that she'd agreed to let him give her a ride home. In the car, he suggested that they go meet his cat in his apartment, but she couldn't be persuaded. To keep hold of him, though, she fellated him beneath the steering wheel. And he'd had to pee terribly. Afterward, he raced her home, then to his home to piss, piss-s-s-s, Oh God! Pissing with his gray cat winding a figure eight around and between his legs, back and forth, purring, purring.

Upon an evening, he'd tripped up her stairs ready to run with her to the Animated Film Festival to see cartoons. But they fucked instead, and the condom came off after he had come. She didn't seem to care, pulling it out of her vagina stretching and smacking, the opposite of a rubber glove yanked off a surgeon's hand. She never seemed to mind on the occasions when he climaxed and she didn't. He could never understand that.

They dressed and just as they were ready to go down the stairs, her roommate ran up and cried at him, "What you don't know is that I really love her!" They left her in tears, and he was stunned, like seeing the boss's son kiss another man.

"So, what do you think?" she'd said.

"About what?" he'd said.

"About my being bisexual?"

"I just don't want to get shot," he'd said, and they laughed that hollow serious laugh all the way to the Film Festival. The last night, she told him about a problem she was having at work, and he'd made the mistake of pointing out that she could be the one in the wrong. She dumped him with a parting shot about how he hadn't listened to her as usual, since like always he had taken up eighty percent of the conversation. He'd been stunned again.

The boss's son's sister had dumped him, too, for his saying some stupid sexist remark. He'd been nervous about dating the boss's daughter, anyway, which is why he'd said it, unaware of what he was saying.

The ghost glided through him. A bite rippled up his legs and spine, sending his body hair straight out like a wave of rain breaking rigidly down a street marking a thunderstorm.

Their remarks had surprised him, which scared him. If you didn't know what you were saying when you said things, and suddenly you had to fear expressing feelings that you didn't know you had, then what could you say, what could you think?

The boss's son was suddenly dead at the age of 31, of AIDS hushed voices rumored, though the papers never did say. The boss died later in a car accident overseas. His widow, whom he'd hadn't loved for decades, wrote an autobiography about how hard it was, how hard to deal with her son being gay. Ecstatic.

Was it his ghost he faced? Or a person of color, a Black phys ed instructor in college whom he'd inadvertently slighted by directing questions to his White assistant even when the Black man eagerly answered, anxious to inform him? Wayne hadn't meant to insult him, he was too awed to talk to a full professor, even a gym teacher. But would he have been, had he been so shy of White professors?

Was it the spirit of some woman he'd disappointed in the past whose love he'd broken, extinguished? Could it be all of them in one bodiless host, a Black, African American, Jewish, gay, lesbian, guy, woman, searching, searching for a place to be or a person to be in his eyes? Why his eyes? Who am I to be sought by a ghost?

I still am who I am, who I was. I am Wayne Benoit, Caucasian, five-ten, 158, thirty-seven, with an above-average income earned through work easier than it's worth. I vote Republican, but I'm no Libertarian, and I believe that we need to help people who need help. I hate bad drivers but admit that sometimes I do some pretty stupid stuff on the highway myself. But of course, when I do, it's different, he laughed.

You nigger, you.

Wayne crumpled. He held his head in his hands, swaying. He remembered Ellen asking him if he knew how important it was to her to have a bris, that she could accept naming the baby Rene, but that for her, the traditional of circumcision was life-giving, vital.

He'd laughed. He cajoled her about putting this barbaric bloody practice next to the worthy Jewish traditions of aspiring to maintain the highest standards of achievement, education, the arts, family values, generosity, the righteous life, as good as good a people can be. They save others in spite of their own self, he'd said, admonishing her with chapter and verse, all of which he had learned from her. He'd gone along with the wedding, the chuppah, the wine glass—not even nitpicking at the fact that she broke her own glass, too, in violation of her people's strict tradition, that was fine. But he wasn't about to endorse a gory ritual that would put his son at risk with only a mohel to sue, when they could be suing an entire hospital if they screwed up and cut his kid's schwantz off.

There had been no bris. He'd beat her down with logic in a place in which logic had no place. Things hadn't lasted much longer after that.

So, was this a future ghost staring him in the face, into his soul, his son's spirit grown the past few years without him?

He moved over to his old desk and pulled open the top drawer to look at the announcement just received of Rene's bar mitzvah just past. And he knew that what he'd said back then had been bullshit, all, utter and complete, used any which way whenever to get his own way, which had been paramount always.

Ellen had seen it, his underlying overall xenophobia, that fabulous parochial defense mechanism she'd seen in him long before he'd seen it in himself.

Gone now, Wayne thought, sighing, crying. All gone and only just, but gone forever, too. Failed, wrong, and gone. So, now what?

For once, he could care less about the ghost.

The ghost sat upon his chest and he saw the body crumble like in a cheap vampire film, first skin to raw flesh, hair fading to stony bone, giant teeth gripped in a grim, lipless smile, humorless, disintegrating, blowing away to dust, dust blown away, wood ash in the wind. Who was it, Black, man, White, woman? The recognition caused him to grin, grim, humorless, smiling full with great yellow teeth and Grand Guignol humor out of a chalky white mandible.

The ghost came into his life like a life-giving breath and stole his soul away to a different sort of celestial place that he had never dreamed of before.

Layover

Jerry never bothered to make a room reservation when he stopped over in Vegas. Vegas is for gambling, he'd say, and gamble he would, all night long. Not that he was a pro or an addict. He held down a job that paid well, buying chips for Atmospheric Commodities back in Raritan, which meant a lot of trips to Silicon Valley and plenty of opportunities to catch a night or a weekend on the Strip. When he dropped into town, he was there to have a good time, totally, he'd say. So, who needed a room when you could sleep on the plane back?

Which is how he ended up at the O.K. Cafe one dawn, a favorite spot of Vegas regulars for eating riptide breakfasts. Jerry was on his way over to the Cafe with two other guys, sales reps for some outfit in New York. They were drunk and he was just sodden. Ralph, the porky short one, jostled against the taller Bernard.

"Goddamn, Bernie, do I always have to prop you up when we go drinking?" An aside to Jerry, "Can't take the fucker anyplace."

"Prop me up?" said Bernard indignantly, "You dumb son of a bitch, you can't even zip up your fly after a piss, you're so wasted. Don't give me that shit."

Ralph grinned and rolled his tongue out, "Bernardo's mad, here, because he takes one drink and his peter goes limp."

Bernard turned to face Ralph directly. "What are you, fucking crazy?" he shouted, glaring down at Ralph.

"Are my prices insane?" Ralph murmured.

"I can drink a fuckin' fifth straight and still pole vault on my thing," said the tall, dark-haired salesman. "You couldn't get a piss hard-on stone cold sober with your little pork link if your life depended on it."

Eyes nearly closed, Ralph waved his hand at Bernard to signify his tried patience. "When will you ever return to reality, Bernadino? I was planking cheerleaders in alphabetical order thirty years ago while you were making love to the palm of your hand in the bathroom, your mama screamin' at the door, 'It's a sin, Bernie, a sin'!"

"Bull-shit! And, it's Bernard!"

When the two of them started to take turns poking each other in the chest with their fingers, Jerry wandered off to a nearby topless club named Mickey's. He slid onto a stool at the bar and ordered an Irish coffee. The bartender turned to make his drink, and Jerry swiveled around to look out the large front window at the two men, still standing in the gutter, arguing still.

He shook his head, "Where do they get the energy?"

He rotated his seat the other way, barking his knees on the bar in the process because the seat didn't do a full 360 degrees. Noting its rectangular fixed back, he cursed the makers of such a stupid chair.

The interior of the bar looked like any Sheraton club room except for the slots along the far end. Dark, fabric-covered walls in cherry complemented the black Naugahyde seats at the red-clothed tables. The bar itself was covered by brown, textured Naugahyde, and it curved around to a small alcove in the rear where three-piece bands played. The stage was empty now, as was the whole place except for the two waitresses. One lounged at the bar opposite the bandstand, leaning against the jukebox, smoking. The other sat at one of the tables figuring out her tips.

His drink arrived and he grabbed it, using the cocktail napkin as a potholder. He eased himself off the stool and drifted over to the plate glass, peering between the reversed, backward letters of Mickey's. Ralph and Bernard were still in the street, but no longer shouting at each other. Holding the drink in his left hand, Jerry leaned his head against his right arm resting on the window and watched the darkness rise.

"Hey, buddy, gimme a break, will you?"

He turned questioningly to the bartender.

"I clean that window."

Class place thought Jerry as he made his way over to one of the tables close by. He sprawled in a chair and drained the coffee while gazing at the endless conversation outside.

"Want another, mister?"

He looked up to stare at two nipples at the end of two sloping breasts eyeing him. Pear-like, he thought, nice. He continued his upward gaze and met an open face of honey complexion, big brown eyes, orange-blond dyed hair. One small chip was missing from a front tooth, very endearing, he thought, cute.

"Another Irish coffee?"

He debated, then said, "No thanks. Maybe later."

"Oh, okay, well if you do want something, just ask Beth over there, 'cause I'm going off now."

He looked at her again, debated again, then said, "Fine. I'll do that."

"Okay, bye," she started to leave.

"Wait," he said. He pulled out a fiver and handed it to her.

"Hey, thanks," she said and he waved a hand languidly at nothing.

"Okay then, bye again," she said as she left.

"Yup, bye."

An apricot border had formed at the sky's low end, and the gray displayed a tint of blue. Ralph unconsciously put his hands up to shade his eyes. Bernard seemed to suggest something, gesturing toward the Cafe with one hand. They both looked around, Ralph shrugged, and they started walking toward the Cafe. Soon, several yards separated their paths.

"Looks like your friends are leaving."

Jerry peered around at the woman who'd spoken, away from the jukebox now but still holding her cigarette. She stood two tables from him, leaning her hip against a third and staring out the window. Her free arm crossed over her breast, not modesty, he knew. Vegas always ran the air conditioning on High.

"Time for me to go?" he asked.

She smiled slightly, "Not if you don't want to." She dropped her arm to stoop and stub out the cigarette. "What can I get you?"

"Oh, nothing. No, wait, how about orange juice? Can you get me that?"

"Sure," she said, and walked back to the bar. As she moved, he thought, also nice. Little apples, not pears. He dwelled on the S curve of her back, not an ounce of fat. Women don't have love handles, he mused, their asses are their love handles.

She returned, "Here you are. I just thought you might not want to miss them, is all."

"What?"

"The other two guys."

"Oh. No, I don't know them. I just met them in the last casino. Couple of traveling salesmen."

"I see."

Her eyes were big, blue pupils with blue-tinted whites, like liquid robins' eggs. She was pretty, he could see, sharp edges to dark, soft lips, which made him wonder how she could end up in a dump like this. Stupid, he supposed. But she didn't look it, her expression looked sharp. Fucked up then, took too many wrong turns in the road. Supporting a jackass boyfriend, maybe?

"You're not a salesman," she stated more than asked.

Ah. Hooking on the side, maybe. Nice brown hair, nice tan, not too overdone, the local's prerogative.

"No, I'm a buyer. I buy computer chips in quantity for a company in the East. I'm just on my way back from California."

"I see," she said.

He looked into her eyes, pointedly away from her boobs. Women like that, he thought. That is, they liked it better than if you stared at their boobs. It probably didn't matter to her, though.

"So, what about you, Beth? What do you do? Other than waitressing, I mean."

Her big eyes shut down a bit. "Oh, you mean am I really an actress or a dancer?" She shook her head, "No, I don't do any of those things. I'm left-footed and I can't act serious in church. No, I'm just a cocktail waitress."

"I see," he said, just then aware that he echoed her. He looked down at the table and rolled the edge of the wet napkin under his juice. He lifted his sight to her eyes. "Can you sit down?"

She smirked a bit, "No."

"I see," he said, quickly following with, "Unhuh. Well, when do you get off?"

Her smirk seemed to broaden. "Six."

"That's about an hour. Want to go on a date?"

She said, "Not really."

"Oh, c'mon," he said, "I just told you my 1ife story."

She laughed.

"There you go," he said. "Who knows? If you go out with me, maybe we'll fall in love, get married, have kids, and divorce all before my plane leaves this morning."

She laughed again, not heartily, but friendly.

"So, what do you say?"

"What do you have in mind?"

"How about breakfast?"

Her smile disappeared businesslike, "I eat breakfast at ten. In the evening."

"Okay, no breakfast. But we can think of something." He looked at her imploringly, as though this was the most important request of his life. She seemed to mull it over in her mind, then said, "All right."

"Great! Where shall I meet you?"

"Right here, six-thirty. Give me a chance to get changed."

His eyes widened in mock surprise, and she laughed, "It takes longer to get into clothes then out of them, jerk."

"Sure, sure, here at six-thirty. I just have to make one phone call." She moved her head back, then relaxed when he said, "To change my flight. I usually leave on the eight fifty-five."

"Okay," she said evenly, "six-thirty."

"Terrific!"

He stood up to leave, and the bartender yelled, "Mac," waving his bill in the air.

"Right," said Jerry, pulling out his wallet. He looked at Beth, thought better of it, and walked to the bar to pay the bill. He walked back to the table and laid down an exact tip.

"My name's Jerry, by the way."

She nodded, "Jerry."

He pointed at her, "Six-thirty."

"Yeah, yeah," she giggled, "six-thirty."

He headed over to the OK Cafe. Ralph and Bernard were in the middle of eggs, potatoes, and toast. Ralph slopped egg yolk and potatoes onto a wedge of toast covered with jam and shoved it into his mouth. Bernard cut his food into precise squares and popped them into his mouth rapid fire. He was nearly finished when Jerry walked in.

Ralph spotted Jerry and shifted the mass of food in his mouth to one side. "Jerry! We missed you terribly! Sit down, sit down," he gestured grandly with his fork.

Jerry sat down. A waitress came over and he ordered toast and coffee, black.

"You don't look so good, Jerry," Bernard said. "Anything the matter?"

Jerry put his head in his hands and said, "Oh, I'm tired and boozy. I'm ready to go to bed."

Ralph said, "Don't worry, we'll fix that. The night's young."

"Day. It's daytime," said Bernard.

"Better yet, it's a brand new day, a new beginning. We've got the other side of the drag to do."

"Yeah, but I'm beat," Jerry mumbled.

"Nonsense. A little drink will fix that, it'll revitalize you. Look, here's your breakfast."

The waitress set down the plate, cup, and saucer. Jerry took one look at the black coffee and said "Can I have some cream and sugar?"

"It's on the table."

"Oh." As he reached, he noticed the gray stubble on Ralph's cheeks, reminding him of the Duke or the Dauphin out of *Huckleberry Finn*. Bernard's long, bleary-eyed face reminded him of no one.

"Eat up," said Ralph, "and we'll be on our way. We can hit the joints one by one, a single bet at each table, do the whole line of them before twelve."

"My plane's at eight fifty-five."

"Bad luck, old man! Can you change it? If not, I heard there's a limo service that's got cars with slots in the rear seats. You can play right up to the ramp!"

"I'm not sure I want to change my flight."

Ralph's smile disappeared. "I see. Is it the company you object to, perhaps? "

"Well, yes. I mean, no, I—"

"For Christsake!"

"Relax, Ralph," said Bernard, "this guy's totaled. Look at him."

"Up yours, Bernard, the guy's a schmuck. He's not wimping out on us, he's—"

"Wait a minute, wait a minute," Jerry cried. "It's not you guys. It's just that, if I change my flight, I have another appointment."

They stared at him.

He sighed, "A date."

The two salesmen looked at each other in open-mouthed surprise, then back at Jerry.

"A date!" said Ralph, "Well, why didn't you say so? That's different. Of course you'll change your flight, and of course we understand. A date!"

"When did you have time to make a date?" Bernard asked pointedly.

Jerry pressed his lips together, then said, "In the bar next door." He rolled his eyes in that direction. "A waitress."

"No shit?" Bernard said, "What a fuckin' guy!"

Ralph ran his hand over his head and said, "A date. My hair's a mess and I can't get me no dates." He turned to Jerry, "So, what's she like, this little strudel you're gonna boff? She a hooker?"

"I don't know. Maybe. "

"They're all hookers here," Ralph said with authority.

"Shit! Fifteen minutes and this guy's got a date," Bernard muttered, shaking his head.

"She's got to be a hooker."

"That's what I'm afraid of," said Jerry.

"Nonsense, nothing to it. You've got the freight, right? I saw you at the tables, you weren't losing much. Anyway, they take credit cards. Isn't that right, Bernard?"

"How the fuck should I know?" Bernard said.

"Why, Bernadette, we all know that it's the only way you can get laid."

"Bullshit! Goddamn it, you fat little shit, I—"

"Control yourself, Bernard. Jerry, here, needs the wealth of your experience."

"I don't know anything about hookers!" He turned to Jerry. "Christ, if you didn't know, why'd you ask her out?"

"I don't know. We were talking, and I wanted to, I guess."

Ralph said, "She's a looker, isn't she?" Jerry nodded and Ralph murmured, "A hooker who's a looker. So, what difference does it make?"

"I never paid for it before."

"You've come to Vegas, how many times, and you never paid for it?"

"I never got laid in Vegas before."

Ralph sat back, draping one arm over the edge of the booth. "Oh. A fluke."

Bernard said, "Come off it, Ralph. When did you ever get laid in Vegas for free?"

"Once. By my ex-wife—before we were exed."

"I feel for you, Jerry. She seemed pretty nice, huh?" Bernard asked.

Jerry thought, then bobbed his head up and down, "Yeah, she did."

"Too bad."

The men were silent for a time. Ralph looked at his wristwatch and began to fidget. After a while, he said, "Well, Jerry, the moment of truth is at hand. There's only one way to find out if she turns tricks, and Bertram and I must go now if we're to lay waste to this wasteland before our plane leaves. What's it gonna be?"

"Shit, I don't know."

"Okay, if you decide to stay but not for your date, you'll find us on the shady side of the street. Let's go, Bernard."

Jerry stood up to let Ralph slide out. The two salesmen left, and he sat down again. Fuck, he thought, it probably would be horrible. He looked up at the clock. Six-thirty. He sighed and sipped his coffee, the bitterness of it making him grimace. He sat for fifteen minutes more, then paid his bill.

The super-heated air outdoors caused him to false step. He clenched his eyelids tightly shut against the sunlight, which masked the blue sky a bright yellow. Another Vegas summer day, he thought, reminding him of why he usually left on a red-eye before sunrise.

He was waiting at the curb for a cab to come by when she stepped out of Mickey's front door. She saw him, frowned, and said, "Did I say to wait out here? It's a lot better inside."

"Oh, I guess I misunderstood," he said. She wore white Levis and a loose, lightly patterned, light blue cotton shirt. Her hair fell free in a flip just above her shoulders, the pointed ends seeming to accent the finely shaped corners of her mouth. How could he forget such details in only an hour, he wondered.

Her eyes lidded over in sudden realization. "Oh. I see," she said. "I'll just catch a bus home."

"Wait a minute," he said, "I got talking to those other two guys and . . . I was going to stand you up."

She nodded, "I know. It' okay. I'm glad you did, no bullshit."

She didn't seem to be angry at all. As she turned to go, he said mournfully, "Now I'm sad I did it."

She turned her head skyward and back to him and said, "Look, what are you doing? Why are you jerking me around like this? You know, I make it a point not to go out with out-of-town guys like you. Couldn't we just forget it?"

"Well, I did. I had amnesia."

A furrow appeared in her head as she looked at him doubtfully, skeptically.

"No, really, I'm okay now, but it was terrifying not knowing who I was, where I came from. It lasted an hour and a half, but it seemed like forever. Then, it all came back to me, but only at six-forty-five."

She tilted her head, half-smiling, shaking her head in amused disbelief. He moved closer to her, lightly touching her arm for emphasis, "I knew who I was at six-forty-five. I was . . ." he finished slowly, "an asshole."

She laughed out loud, bending a little at the waist.

"What do you say?" Jerry said, "let's give it a shot."

She lifted her shoulders and dropped them, smirking again, "I was ready before. Okay. What'll we do?"

He put his hand to his mouth. "Gee, I don't know. But I do have to phone and change that flight."

They left, laughing.

In bed, they stared together at the ceiling of her apartment, all white like the walls, no painting or nail marks from pictures, please. Beth had photos and reproductions and Afghans all over the place anyway.

"I've lived here six years," she said, "how am I supposed to call it home without a few pictures on the walls?"

How could she ever call it home? But then he thought about the dump he lived in, what they called a railroad apartment, a string of rooms one leading into the next without a picture or curtain in sight. He glanced away to the glass doors of the balcony overlooking the swimming pool, unoccupied. Vivid sunshine split the half-drawn drapes and the gauzy curtains. A woman's touch, he thought.

"Gotta pee," she said, bouncing out of the bed to the bathroom. He could see a crack of light and hear the trickle through the partially shut door. He heard the flush and watched her return to the bed. With all of her clothes off, the rubbery tawdry look of her breasts in Mickey's was gone, replaced by the curves natural to women unadorned, art status of antiquity. Only the whiteness of her skin where her bathing suit covered her disrupted the illusion.

She caught him looking at her and said, "Hungry?"

"Maybe. What have you got to eat?"

"Whole-wheat pita bread, tofu, lots of vegetables, bean sprouts—I could make you a good sandwich."

"Pita bread? Tofu? You're a health food nut. How come you smoke?"

She plopped down on the side of the bed and reached for a cigarette, "Just one of my little personal contradictions. I smoked a long time before I ate natural foods." She lit up and exhaled, "I'll quit someday."

"Sure you will," he said. "Well, I'll pass on dinner, thanks."

"Oh, steak and spuds man, huh?"

He smiled sheepishly, "Yeah, I guess."

She leaned toward him and said enthusiastically, "Let me make you a sandwich. They're really good!"

"Okay," he said skeptically.

She padded off. He put his hands behind his head, elbows splayed. He could still taste the acrid sweetness of her mouth. He shook his head, cigarettes. Yet, they'd made pretty good love together, even with the condom. Which, he admitted to himself, he'd been both glad and disappointed about at the same time. Still, it'd been pretty good. The odd feel of new shapes of a new body had been there, the difference in desire—-techniques they'd call them in some sex how-to books. But they were comfortable together.

He liked her. They'd had a good time goofing around downtown. Peeking in at a show, she'd kidded him about the boobs on the showgirls. When he grandiosely put down a hundred bucks on a table and lost it at one turn, she'd walked away saying she didn't know him. She was fun. The only bad moment came when they ran into Ralph and Bernard, the sons of bitches. They were supposed to be in the joints on the shady side of the street.

"But there is no shade in Vegas," Ralph pleaded cheerfully. "Nice to meet you, little lady."

He eyed her openly, up and down. Bernard was no better. Jerry could sense himself getting pissed off when Bernard took him aside.

"Well, what's the story?"

"What do you mean, Bernard?"

"I mean, is she or isn't she?"

"I don't know."

"Oh, come on! You've been with her long enough to fuck her ten times over. Let a guy know, for Christsake."

"Bernard, listen—"

"How's it going, boys?" Ralph said. "Jerry, she's a real winner, hooker or not. Boy, would I like to see those milkers unwrapped! If only I'd gone into that bar instead of you!"

"Ralph, what the fuck?" Jerry said.

"Ralph, Jerry here says he still hasn't laid her yet."

"What? Well, move over, boy, I got a one-fifteen plane to catch."

Ralph turned to go, but Jerry grabbed him by the arm and spun him around, watching for Beth, who leaned against a low wall, waiting patiently.

"Listen, asshole!" Jerry hissed sharply.

"Asshole? You're the asshole. Shit or get off the pot, son."

"What the fuck do you think you're doing, Jerry?" Bernard said loudly, "You were the one who wanted to split 'cause you thought she was a whore! Don't start this noble boyfriend crap now!"

Livid, Jerry dropped Ralph's arm. "Whether she's a whore or not, she's with me and I don't want you two motherfuckers fucking with her while I'm around!"

"Oh yeah, well fuck you!" shouted Bernard.

People began to gather at the edge and Ralph started to shift nervously from foot to foot. He placed a hand on one of Bernard's arms and said, "Cool down, Bernard, let's not make trouble. The man's right, he found her first."

"You bet your ass I'm right!" Jerry said.

"Let's leave them alone so he can have his fun with her."

They began to walk away and the people watching went back to their drinks and the tables. Jerry slowly moved to rejoin Beth when he heard Ralph say, "When we come back through Vegas next week, we'll just go over to Mickey's ourselves and line up the little lady for a little train ride, that's all."

Jerry pivoted around, but Beth pulled at him. "Hey," she said, "let's go someplace else."

"Those fucking assholes!"

"Here's your sandwich."

He sat up, took one bite, and an explosion of good taste crowded his mouth with released juices. "Good God!" he said fervently, "This is wonderful! What's in it?"

"Oh, avocado, bean sprouts, tofu— that's bean curd— and cheese. Oh, and homemade mayo."

"Well, it's great. Bean curd, huh?" He took another huge bite and said in a muffled voice, "You should open up a restaurant."

"Sure. Here in Las Vegas. We'll call it The Roulade Wheel. All I need is a grubstake."

"No, no, I mean you could really do it."

She said, "Not me. I'm not into food preparation."

She finished her sandwich and rolled over beside him, picking stray bean sprouts off her breasts and belly. "I'm such a slob."

He munched quietly for a while, looking at her. She glanced up and saw his thoughtful gaze and said, "I know. You want to know how I got here, ended up where I am at Mickey's."

He nodded, "Let me guess. Early marriage to a jerk. Gone was all your money and gone was he."

"Yeah, except he wasn't a jerk, he was a shithead."

"An important detail."

"Right."

"So, where are you from?"

"Right here."

"You're kidding? You mean you're a local girl?"

"You got it. Born, raised, and deflowered in the shadow of Las Vegas High. Married at eighteen, divorced at twenty-two."

He continued nodding as he listened. "So, see your folks much?"

"No, they moved."

"Where to?"

"Can you believe it, Atlantic City of all places. Home away from home." They laughed together.

He finished his sandwich, tidying up his fingers with his tongue. "One appetite down and one to go."

Bulging his eyes out, he reached for her.

"Wait a minute, not so fast," she said, avoiding his grasp. "You forgot one little thing."

"What?"

"My ten thousand dollars," she said.

What? he thought. Then he said evenly, "What do you mean?"

"My ten thousand dollars. You said you'd give me ten thousand dollars. Now, where is it?"

She was half-smiling until she saw him sit back against the pillows. "What's the matter? I say something wrong?"

"No, no," he said hurriedly.

"Well then, what's the problem?" She leaned over to hug him, "Come on, it's a small sum."

He pressed his 1ips in a grimace, not responding to her.

She sat up. "Say, you're really bothered by something. What's wrong? C'mon, tell me."

"It's nothing," he said, but he could see she wasn't buying. "Well, it's something I thought, then didn't think was so, then I did. I don't know."

She looked completely bewildered.

He said, "It has to do with my almost standing you up this morning." She remained puzzled, so he added, "And those two jerks at Caesars."

"What, your two salesmen buddies? I'm not following you."

"It has to do with a conversation we had, a discussion about . . . you."

"Me?" she said, touching her breastbone with one finger. Then her expression changed, like dawn. "Oh. I think I'm getting the picture. You didn't know whether you wanted to go out with me or not because—I see. All that shit with those two in the hotel makes sense now." She looked at him with laughter in her eyes, "What were you doing, defending me?"

He made a face, lifting, then dropping his hands.

"Jesus, what a great guy," she laughed, punching him on the arm.

"Yeah," he said glumly.

"You're still wondering," she said. "You still don't know. My joke about the ten thousand dollars started it all up in you again."

He said nothing.

"All right," she said, "ask me. Don't look so surprised, you want to know, so ask me."

She crossed her arms over her breast and waited. He didn't say anything for a time, then finally, in a tentative voice, he said, "Are you?"

"Am I what?" she snapped.

He flinched, but said, "A hooker. Are you a hooker?"

She didn't answer right away, once more debating in her mind. Then, she uncrossed her arms, and a small smile played at those sharp corners of her mouth.

"Sometimes," she said.

"Sometimes? What do you mean 'sometimes'? I don't understand how you can be a hooker sometimes."

"It's simple. I go out with guys I like. Sometimes they give me money. Like you, they don't know, but they don't ask, unlike you. It's simpler for me just to keep it."

"Oh. I see. Well, then."

She snuggled up to him. "Hey. You don't owe me a thing. I should pay you," she said.

He smiled at that. Then he said, "I better call for a cab and get to the airport."

"We've got time," she said shifting over him. "I'll drive you."

The dry wind blew through her hair on the way to the airport, displaying another aspect of her attractiveness. She drove a vintage convertible, of course. He wondered if she'd bought it not conscious of the way it caused a breeze to sweep through her hair. She wore the same white Levis as before but sported a lime-green terry cloth halter top, which accented those fine apples. Not pears. Abruptly, he asked, "You have any kids?"

"Nope." She formed her lips into a tight smile and said, "I spend it all on myself."

The air was still hot despite the wind blowing by the car. He felt fatigue suddenly wrap itself around him. They drove silently for a while, looking straight ahead. Finally, she broke the silence.

"So, how's your job, Jerry?"

"It's a shit job. I'm bored with it, mostly."

"Is that why you come here?"

"Yeah. I guess."

They arrived at the airport and after parking the car they walked to the locker where he had stashed his bags. She helped him carry them to the security line. He dropped the bags at the end of the zigzagging line, and she pulled him aside. "Well, I had a nice time," he said.

"Yeah. Listen, you're a nice guy, you know? You're straight with people, you know what I mean? So, look, when you stop over in Las Vegas again, if you'd like to go out, you know, have a few laughs? Maybe a meal. Anyway, I wrote my name and number on this piece of paper. If you feel like it, look me up, give me a call. It was nice."

She grasped him behind the nape of his neck, pulled him down to her level and kissed him firmly on the lips.

"Bye, Jerry," she said. She skipped out of the terminal.

Bye, he thought, the press of her lips still on his. The hair on his neck tingled from her touch, and he rubbed it until the sensation was gone. He opened the slip of paper with both hands and read.

Mary Beth Cole
867 Bluebird Ct., Apt. 2E
Las Vegas, Nevada 89121
702-367-2912

Mary Beth. He crumpled the paper and stuffed it into the side pocket of his jacket. He passed through security and retrieved his bags. Slinging them over his shoulders, he headed for his gate at a trot.

On the way, he saw Ralph and Bernard sitting in plastic chairs at their gate. Ralph looked done in, and Bernard hovered over him impatiently.

Ralph, his elbows on his knees, his hands supporting his head, spied him first. "Hello, Jerry. You still pissed at us?"

Jerry shook his head no.

"Good. I was drunk. I am drunk. Now I'm sick."

Bernard, with some hostility remaining behind his eyes, turned to see Jerry.

"Can't stop," Jerry said, "plane's already boarding."

"Right," said Ralph. "One thing. Is she a hooker?"

He stopped at that. He glanced at them both, then put his hands in his jacket pockets. "No, she isn't."

"Oh, bullshit," Bernard muttered, "you just don't want to admit you had to pay for it."

Rolling the crumpled paper around in his pocket, Jerry said, "You're right. She's a hooker."

"What'd I say," Bernard said, twisting his head away, "they're all whores here."

Jerry started to walk and was ten feet away when he heard Ralph exclaim, "Wait a minute. She wasn't a hooker?"

"Oh, bullshit," Bernard said wearily.

On the plane next to a window, Jerry shaded his eyes from the glare of the bright light. He stared out at the stained gray concrete for a time until the plane began to taxi for takeoff. Then, he drew the blind halfway down and rested his head back against his airline pillow.

A handsome flight attendant, her hair short-cut fair and fine like corn silk, strapped herself into a seat facing the passengers three rows down. She yawned, just covering with one hand the muted silver of the braces punctuating her even white smile. He stifled his own yawn and pinched his dry tear ducts to relieve his tiredness. Soon, she'd be around with drinks, he thought, if he could last that long. The plane began its lumbering ascent into the yellow sky, exerting to push through the shimmer of hot air beneath the blinding white sun.

Résumé

282 South Street
Williamstown, PA
08102
June 6th, 1983

Dorectpr pf Juman
Resource Management

Shit.

282 South Street
Williamstown, PA
08102
June 6th, 1983

Director of Human
Resource Management
Thc Konig Company
1413 L Street, N.W.
Suite 1200
Washington, D.C.
20016

Dear Madam or Sir,

Your advertisement in The Washington Post for an ediotr—

—editor

```
piqued my interst—
```

Shit.

```
                  —interest.  I beleive—
```

Shit.

```
—believe my experience and background to be
eminently well-suited to this position, and I
weold—
```

Shit!

```
                          —would like to
explore with you this opportunity of
employment toward our mutual beneift.—
```

God-dammit!

At the Polo Grounds, the Teetotalers are being mugged by the Gashouse Gorillas. The Gorillas dance around the bases in a Conga line, each refrain punctuated by the sound of a hit off of a bat, "dah-dah, dah-dah, dah crack! Dah-dah, dah-dah, dah crack!" One Teetotaler fields a line drive, which pushes him back under a mound of dirt topped by daisies and a tombstone. The Umpire bellows "Ball!" and the Gorilla catcher punches him into the ground. The Umpire staggers to his feet and changes the call to a strike.

Wearing a straw skimmer and a striped jacket, holding a bag of popcorn in one hand and a carrot in a bun in the other, Bugs Bunny catcalls from a hole in the infield, saying he could beat them Gorilla bums single-handed. A stubble-bearded Gorilla with a stogie in his mouth eyeballs Bugs and says, "You're on!" Bugs gulps.

In a uniform labeled "Brooklyn," Bugs throws warm-up pitches to himself. Behind a catcher's mask and pad, he pounds his mitt, calling for the ol' pepper, the hot mustard, the big-league stuff—the ball knocks him into the backstop. He stalks back, chattering for the ol' pepper, the hot mustard, the big-league stuff. The ball knocks him into the backstop.

A huge Gorilla comes to the plate. A little fellow wearing a uniform with "Bat Boy" stenciled on the back flies in on bat wings and hands the Gorilla a bat. The Gorilla swings it menacingly. A pitch comes, and Bugs flashes a 1940's girlie poster. The batter whistles and howls like a wolf, and the Umpire calls a strike.

Bugs says, "I t'ink I'll perplex 'im wit me slow ball." The batter fans one, two, three times at a single pitch.

In the bottom of the ninth, the scoreboard reads Bugs Bunny 96, Gashouse Gorillas 95, with a Gorilla on base and two outs. The batter chops down a tree and uses its trunk as a bat. Bugs decides to use his pachydermish pitch and winds up accompanied by the noise of a gyroscope. The Gorilla crushes the ball, which opens a screaming mouth as it goes out of the ballpark. Bugs rushes out and hales a taxi to go to the Umpire State Building. But the driver is a Gorilla who takes Bugs the wrong way. Bugs races out of the cab to the waterfront, swims to the Statue of Liberty, climbs up and throws his glove up to catch the ball from the torch. The Umpire sticks his head out of her crown and says to a Gorilla on the statue's shoulder, "Yer out!" The Statue leans over and wags her finger at the complaining Gorilla, saying, "That's what the man said!"

```
    At present, I am self-employed as a free-lance
ediotr-
```

Shit.

```
             -editor and writer. Most recently, I
    worked for seven and a half years as a Senior
    Ediotr-
```

"Oh, Goddamn it."

-Editor in the Corridor Press, Inc. Magazine Division, until I left in March to write fiction and to travel extensively. At Coridor, I commissioned numerous articles on a wide variety of self-help topics, including alternative sources of energy, renewable agriculture, health and fitness. The excellence of these articles demanded a hands-on approach that invovled-

-involved me in all aspects of their development, including proposals, author contracts, and copyediting. I also supervised art design and illustrations, and aided with promotion and production.

Mr. Rogers visits Handyman Negri and asks him to show us how to repair the handle on a broken shovel. Handyman Negri extracts the studs and the split haft from the shovel head and fits a new haft into the neck. He hammers in two bolts and the shovel is as good as new.

In the Magic Kingdom, King Friday discovers a $3,000 surplus in the Kingdom's budget. He decrees that a community swimming pool shall be built and that all of his loyal subjects will help with the excavation. Lady Eberline wears a hardhat with a light and the puppets wear little hardhats with little lights.

Mr. Rogers feeds his fish, one shake, two shakes. He changes his slippers for shoes, his sweater for a jacket, and leaves, singing about how there is only one of "you."

While at Corridor, I also acquired serialization rights to book chapters from subsidiary rights representatives of book publishers. This function afforded me the chance to learn how to accurately conduct and analyze statistical research of high validity as well. I also was able to hone my interpersonal abilities with various personalities. The combination of my responsibilities seasoned my organizational skills through the need to maintain long range magazine schedules for articles while meeting short term crisis deadlines for series acquisition many a time.

Natalie Dearborn furtively approaches Grant Putnam in a General Hospital hallway. She asks in a guarded voice what progress he's made in securing Dr. Gerald's new, cheap-energy device, the Prometheus Disk. Grant coolly tells Natalie to relax, that everything is proceeding according to plan, and that he has matters well in hand. Natalie reminds him that this is Natasha speaking, Comrade, and that he better not forget it. Holding his ire in check, Grant defers to her rank. After they part, she walks over to a pay phone in the hospital lobby to report the conversation to her DBX control.

Luke Spencer continues to ready his casino for its grand opening, but Police Commissioner Scorpio harasses him whenever he can, which leads Luke to consider running for mayor of Port Charles. Black slaps fives with Luke, who has promised him a job. Unknown to Luke, Connie is a WSB agent.

I've enclosed a résumé of my experience and background that will show that my personal interests cover an even wider spectrum of interests, especially traveling. I just recently returned from a two-month journey in the South Pacific, where I kept daily journals of my experiences. Of course, I would welcome the chance of a personal interview to discuss my qualifications further. If you would like to pursue this, I can be reached either at my home telephone number(215-770-5717), or at my brother's residence in Falls church, Virginia, where I spend half of my time (Telephone number: 703-336-4542). Thank you for considering my suggestions.

Sincerely,

Dennis J. McConaghy

282 South Street
Williamstown, PA
08102
September 9th, 1983

Employment Services Department
New England Life
501 Boylston Street
Boston, Massachusetts
002117
Washington, D.C.
20017

Gentlefolk,

I read with keen interest your advertisement in The Boston Sunday Globe for a Writer/Editor. I believe that my experience and background are well-suited to this position, and I would like to explore with you this opportunity of employment toward our mutual benefit.

At present I am self-employed writing fiction, but most recently I held the position of Senior Editor in the Corridor Press Inc. Magazine Division. In this capacity I headed up a staff that produced articles an—

"Shit!"

—on a variety of subjects, including

At a WWII airfield, Bugs lounges on a bomb under the wing of an airplane, reading a book entitled *Winning with Hare Power.* Bugs laughs in ridicule at legendary creatures known as gremlins who "sab-o-tag-e" aircraft in dia . . . diabolical ways." Just then, a tiny gnome with airplane wings instead of ears wearing a leather flight helmet and goggles, begins to tap the nose of the bomb with a large mallet. After watching him tap it a few times, Bugs says, "Annh, what's the hubbub, Bub?"

The little mite tells him that these blockbusters have to be hit just right. Bugs, whispering, asks, "You mind if I take a crack at it?" He eases the gnome aside with his foot, spits on his hand, clutches the mallet, winds up twisting his body twice around, and swings. Millimeters from the nose of the bomb he screeches to a halt and screams, "What am I doing!?!" Then, he says, "Say, do you think . . . could it be . . . could that have been . . . a gremlin?"

The creature flies up and blasts in his ear, "It ain't Vendell Vilkie!" He pulls Bugs' ears to the ground, smashes his foot with a wrench, stands on the plane wing, and smashes him on the head.

282 South Street
Williamstown, PA
08102
December 4th, 1983

Editor/Sports Writer
P.O. Box d3014
Emmettsburg, Maryland
20464

Gentlefolk,

I read with extreme interest your advertisement in The Washington Post for an

Editor/Sports Writer, and I would like toss my hat into the ring. I've had extensive editorial experience in magazine publishing, as my résumé will inform you. However, I believe that my avocational passion for all sports supersedes my professional credentials in this case.

On the 20 Minute Workout, the two girls wear spanking brand new Danskins and de rigueur legwarmers in pastel colors. Their shoes show no signs of wear. Their bodies are from another planet, not products of earthly aerobics.

In close order drill, the girls prance and dance, run in place, swing their arms out and front in remarkable unison. They spread their legs and s-t-r-e-t-c-h, bending at the waist like no man can contemplate. They repeatedly touch their hands to the pure white floor.

The camera moves around them, above them, behind them, demonstrating a hundred different angles from which to fade away just avoiding crotch shots.

Count Digital 19 and cool down close up, exposing a scant scalene of perspiration tracing the V of the front cheerleader's gathered spandex.

Inscribed below on the screen, ~Research offers evidence that a diet rich in fiber can help prevent cancer of the colon. ~

282 South Street
Williamstown, PA
08102
February 8th, 1948

The Washington Post
Box No. M101
1150 15th Street, N.W.

Washington, D.C.
20071

Gentlefolk,

I read with keen interest your advertisement for a Public Relations/Technical Writer. I believe that my professional experience combined with my genuine desire to work on legislative issues for a nonprofit firm would enable me to bring special verve to this post. Hence, I would like to explore with you this employment opportunity toward our mutual benefit.

At present, I am self-employed as a freelance writer and editor. Before this, I worked for more than seven years at Corridor Press, until I left to write fiction and to travel extensively. I've since pursued these goals to my satisfaction, and I'm eager to reenter the professional publishing community. I've enclosed a résumé of my qualifications for your review, which upon first glance might seem too homogenous in nature stemming from seven years with the same company. Since such an impression, along with the expectation that I seek comparable seniority could lead a prospective employer to dismiss my candidacy preemptively (possibly a factor in the length of my present period of self-employment), I urge you to examine closely my varied skills and the myriad ways in which I could contribute to your organization.

While at Corridor Press, I held the position of Senior Editor in their magazine division. In this capacity I headed up a staff that included alternative energy sources, home building projects, health and fitness, gardening, wildlife, and many others. In creating these articles, I was responsible for every facet of their development, among them budgeting, supervising copyediting and art design, and aiding in the final production stages. My series "Wholesome Home Recipes for Household Products" typifies the success enjoyed by my projects in that readers ranked it as the most popular feature in Self Help magazine during each of the six issues in which it ran, spurring a 30 percent increase in circulation as a result.

I might add that not a single lawsuit emerged from the unfortunate comfrey incident, and only a smattering of readers wrote, usually in good humor, of their puzzlement regarding the odd proportions for making tea, (1 c.to 1 oz. herb). Needless to say, these discrepancies received immediate attention and appropriate disclaimers appeared in subsequent issues.

For my own part, I hope to expand my professional horizons in a new arena, which is why I've elected not to return to Corridor. If you care to check my references, you'll find that my employment record confirms the fact that I indeed did resign and that the question "Would you rehire this employee?" will produce the answer "Yes." Of course, if you come away with more than just the record, or worse nothing other than a sense of disquiet from unspoken nuances of disapproval and pity, please remember that accountability in the dissolution of any seven-year affair is difficult to assign. I know that employment inquiries ordinarily omit references to these matters, but I'm also aware that, by its clandestine nature such innuendo otherwise goes undisputed. At this point in my search, I'm ready to take my chances with the possibility of the truth.

The truth: what is the truth? I recognize what's more important to you, you seek profess-ional truth. Perhaps you ask these questions in stern voices, while I must wonder, the need to know, who you've been talking to (or should I say to whom?). Lord knows I want to find out what is what and why the world's turned wrong. But wait, this is not a lament, this is not the wailing and tearing of hair by some latter-day Job. No, no, I spend too much time beating my own breast, Mea Culpa; what do you expect from an Irish Catholic, better yet, a fallen-away, male Irish Catholic? You've heard often enough the homily, "Think of the starving people in Asia." Well, I do, I literally think of them starving and dying, in Southeast Asia of course, the new chapter in the Book of Revelations. Take it a step further: Tom Dimmesdale sheltered a Cambodian Refugee named Try (pronounced Tree) who had been dumped at the Philadelphia Airport in midwinter with $25 and no English. Through a torturous series of circumstances, he wound up at Tom's, where he was so grateful to be alive in an utterly alien world that he washed Tom's car, every day.

The function Try performed was to hold Tom and Judy's new baby all evening long (after first doing the dishes, of course). Holding little Eli comforted Try as much as the baby, since the language barrier assumed natural dimensions.

Possessing general convictions about human dignity, Tom couldn't allow Try to continue washing his car, his dishes, or holding the baby, even if the family had grown used to having a de facto hand servant. He took Try to a local restaurant to see if they needed a busboy, which they didn't. Then, reading the classifieds the next day, Tom found the same restaurant running an ad for busboys.

A cliché, I know, but I swear I'm not making this up, nor the part about the Khmer Rouge's debate in front of Try of whether or not to execute him as they just had his father and brother. Ten years old at the time, he was spared for being politically insignificant. I can’t exaggerate about his joy either at discovering through a cousin’s letter that his mother, whom he’d not seen for two years, was still alive.

Knowing Try and his history, how can I possibly style my misfortunes, my life’s miscues as the story of some human plagued by God? But you see, even this failure of self-pity shades my misery. I can’t even feel sorry for myself, which of course is another way of feeling sorry for myself.

What engendered all of this unprofessional consternation, you might ask? What compares so to Try’s sad life? Many events, beginning with the death of my cat. Stop your laughter, you bastards, he was my cat! Lovers have come and gone but he was always there to comfort me. When I prodded Marie to move out, Fender stayed. Ours was a higher form of love, we communicated without speaking, we shared caresses in bed but without carnal veniality.

Not to say that he held no physical attraction to me. On the contrary, the deep smoke gray of his fur, the exquisite, large feral ears, the perfection of domestic head melded with Siamese length, and the moonlight color of his eyes, eyes the color of time, say the Spanish, moved me, stirred with me continuous wonder and appreciation of his flawless, unthinking creation. Always sublime in appearance, what else but a cat could afford to juxtapose insensitivity and affection, stark stares framed in the softest fur, (hair, rather, that sheds to deflect any coveting of their pelts, cagey evolutionaries that they are). Like all of his kin, he combined never-ending dexterity with a true reprobate’s laziness, a remittance beast. Most of all, cats exercise a superb sense of humor couched in the very best of absurd poses, that of absolute seriousness. My cat Fender demonstrated all of these traits and most endearing of all, my cat reminded me of me.

So, he died of kitty-cat leukemia, his second bout. He was only a cat, for Christ's sake, but the day he died he dragged his sick body one more time into the bathroom to give me my usual morning greeting, noisy like a Siamese, one figure-eight twine between the legs, the furry snake. Man, I loved that cat, but what do you expect after six years? Next to my family, it was the most enduring union I've ever had.

His death augured more of the same, beginning with, and more germane to your concerns, my job. I like to think that you can view my career at Corridor as a curve on a graph with a slow, minimal rise for five years, then two sudden quantum leaps in the next two years followed by a precipitous drop in my fortunes off the face of the chart. This typical rendering, though, neglects the distribution of the credit for the termination of this relationship. Personnel recorded it as a cooperative resignation, which is to say that they kicked me out the door with dollar bills clutched in my fists. The affair embarrassed them as much as it humiliated me.

Shall I say that Sonya, our Fearless Leader, was to blame? Certainly she was no help. Among my peers in the "professional publishing community," as my dear associate Frank Ebersol used to put it, I once quipped that Sonya was the kind of person who never failed to be gracious in someone else's defeat. I knew, though, that my problems with her resided deep down. Sonya liked to express herself in terms such as "challenge," which meant dirty work nearly impossible to do, and "career," which asked the hidden question, "What have you done for me lately?" These words puzzled me.

When my father prepared to leave home for the office, he talked about having to put on his "uniform" to go to "Holy Work." Yet, Sonya believed in career, she was a Saint of the Workplace. I often entertained the sad notion that she buried herself in work as her way of reducing the time all humans spend thinking of the pain of life, and then of death. I pitied her for this and always will, but I was at risk, too.

When she decided that things were wrong with an employee, she believed devoutly that she acted in good faith. So, when she circumspectly asked my proofreaders, production assistants, and my authors if they were having any problems with Dennis, of course she glommed on to their responses as the truth, the whole truth. Never mind that to the grunts she questioned she as the Vice President of Everything merely seemed to them to be asking for some information. They were utterly unaware that they supplied her with specific evaluation ammunition. As for the authors, when has any one of them ever been enamored with the changes made by an editor?

The irony of it was that I could see it happening on schedule, because I'd been a part of the other side. Henry Johanna, Henry Whiteford, all the others had succumbed to this inexorable process, The Question. I recognized it because I remembered her asking me about them! I'd watched nuances turn to neutronium as in some science fiction story, a subtle but damning shift in reality for these men, disappeared, their model gnomes or planes remained, left on their desks. I witnessed the disintegration of their characters, the more severe loss of self-faith rather than simply losing a job. They looked crushed, they looked shaken, the blood left their faces.

Now it was happening to me! I refuted each fault on her list, but my step-by-step protest was dismissed as a well-known over-sensitivity to criticism. My mother often stated that I always contradicted her, and when I said, "Mom, I do not!" she said, "There you go again."

Of course, I contradicted my mother all the time. I left myself open for Sonya's Inquisition, too. I admit, I'd adopted my father's attitude about work and expanded it into an arrogance of unusual proportions. When I first started work at Corridor, I never thought I'd be staying for more than a year, two years at the outside. I never took the place seriously, though ironically, it was a comfortable enough place for me to stay for as long as I did. So, the near disaster of the Wholesome Home Recipes series in *Self Help* magazine became a "career" disaster for me, compounded by my previously having argued Sonya into a promotion and a 40 percent raise (cf. sudden incline, years six and seven on career graph). I'd raised the stakes in the face of a 25+ million-dollar beating Corridor happened to be taking due to the folding of their ill-conceived, ill-fated women's magazine *ME*!. This, too, in the midst of our country's worst recession since the '30s.

I botched the series, first by not checking more carefully the credentials of one contributor recruited by a flaky assistant with whom Sonya had saddled me, one of her personal reclamation projects. This flaky assistant's flaky author liberally strewed comfrey in all of her herbal recipes for internal use, a substance that we subsequently learned contained chemicals similar to some that had caused cancer in rats when force-fed truckloads of the stuff.

No excuse, there, however, as a

promotional copyeditor pointed out to me; Corridor readers had been known to eat truckloads of anything featured in their magazines. I didn't pick up on this gaffe until the first part of the series had reached the galleys stage, ready to run. My flaky assistant had allowed a formula for consumption to list 1 oz. for tea, never once putting together the image of an ounce of comfrey equating in volume to an ounce of grass.

I engineered my second screw-up when I hired another assistant to replace the flake, who had left to teach our young. I engaged Carrie, an ingénue fresh out of Smith, thinking she'd be easy to manage. I assigned her tasks and sat back to mull. She performed them badly, then demanded more responsibility. Yet, in her first review, I wrote a glowing report in order to get her a top-of-the-line raise because Sonya had allotted her a starting salary of only $11,000. But when the crunch on the Recipes series hit, I discovered to my horror that not only did I have my own work to finish, which was severely in arrears I freely confess, I also had to do over all of Carrie's.

I'd screwed up, and Sonya called me on it. All explanations were excuses, and the ultimate success of the series, my series, my idea, the series that put the division back in the black, didn't matter. Neither did the next two projects I completed, both without a hitch. By then it was too late, Sonya's righteous snowball was rolling down the hill. Carrie left to learn computers at a bank, but before so, she'd had several heart-to-hearts with Sonya about my poor managerial style. I'd kept my mouth shut throughout all, knowing I'd hear about the glowing review I'd given Carrie, young Sonya in Sonya's eyes.

We struck a deal and I hung around for three months reading the NY*Times* and waiting for good weather to travel to Australia. I can remember the day I knew I was out, solemnly saying, "This is the only flesh I have upon this firmament, and one thing I can say is that I never bought into their program. They've made an honest man out of me again."

That's it, right? I lost my job, so I'm a mess. Earlier, I pointed out quite poignantly via the fate of the two Henrys that being fired causes a loss of one's confidence in his or her tools to make a basic living, critical in the crowded professional world of the Baby Boom Generation. But it happens all the time; big deal, you think.

Yes, it is and yes it doe; it happened to me, and it happened to my father, too. His immediate superior, a vice president, accused him of being an alcoholic and had him summarily spirited off to a clinic, like a CIA operation. The memory of it shames me now because once I persuaded my brothers and sisters to confront Dad with the possibility that he was an alcoholic, since he drank heavily in the years after Mom's death and I was out of favor. He forgave us for it, he forgave me, but he never forgot the humiliation. He survived the attempt upon his character at work, too, the crowning vindication coming from the president of his company, who asked him to go for a drink as soon as he was discharged.

So, when I told Dad of my leaving Corridor, highlighting the settlement in a breezy manner to keep him from worrying, since by this time he was sick, he frowned. He said in his world-knowing way, "They're after you over there. Someone's out to screw you." I don't think he could've said any other words I needed to hear more at the time. I cavalierly made plans to go to the South Pacific for two months, figuring I might as well since I had nothing else on my plate. But my dad took a turn for the worse, and I didn't know what to do. Then, two weeks before he died, he told me, "Denny, if I die, go to Australia. What good is it going to do me if you don't go, huh? So, go."

I never thought he was going to die then, but then, I never thought he was going to die. It kills me now to think of the pain he went through, not the physical part, though that itself mush have been terrible. When they had him on the catheter, he'd wake up and begin to move out of the bed. I'd hold him, and he'd insist to me urgently, "Denny, I must pee!" and I'd tell him, but what could I tell him?

Worse than this, though, he knew what was happening to himself a year before. When he first got sick, he was too quick not to know where this was leading. In an off-handed way on the phone, he'd said to me wryly, "Well, Denny, you know, I punished the bottle and now it's punishing me." He knew what was happening and he fought it by the book, changing his diet profoundly, giving up drinking utterly after his physician first diagnosed him. Quitting drink was no problem for him, he stopped effortlessly for the two years he lived after his diagnosis. Yet, the head cardiologist at the hospital said to me in a throwaway, "Your father must've drunk up half of Williamstown the shape he's in." I could have strangled the asshole on the spot. But I couldn't, he was supposed to be saving my father's life. And the night before my dad died, completely lucid after a horrifying scare during the last two weeks, he said, "This is a lousy way to live."

We all got to tell him that we loved him, and he, us. I "filched," as he put it, three peppermints for him that last night, the night I almost didn't show up to see him because he seemed so much better. Though, when I arrived, he said impatiently, "Where've you been?" And when I leaned over to kiss him good night, he started, as if at the unknown. Then he said, "Oh. I love you too, Denny."

I left for Australia two weeks later. For some reason, I felt less unsettled by Dad's death than my mom's. My brother and sister had died five years before her, so I'd known that first shock of the death of loved ones. But Mom's suffering scared me, a young man in the fierceness of his twenties witnessing what seemed to be terrible pain ended only by death, a terrifying idea. At thirty-five, I feel closer to Dad, that I'm not that far from the same event that either will join us all again or relieve me of having to think about never seeing them anymore.

I sum up this attitude in one of the many mottos I coined while at Corridor Press: "If I can just make it through the rest of my life, I'll be all right." Another one I often go by is "Excess in moderation."

After Dad, Marie's departure should have seemed anticlimactic. It galls me to think that I cared for her so, though I knew her as a poor bet from the jump. I should have known, too, that she was untrustworthy when one time, thinking that I wasn't looking, she squirreled away behind my back some glass jars I'd consigned irrevocably to recycling. I should have known something was up when she started taping all of my albums.

She left, but not before easing her conscience by telling me about the two guys on her trip to Europe this past fall, and the guy in town while I was off in Australia. She changed me by this, my introduction to the graphic type of betrayal, fish-white forms undulating within known, narrow borders over her amber body. I suffered a sickness of vision and wonder now if jealousy will attend every romance of mine from here on.

Of course, I renounced her in absentia for all of this, thinking to myself, she'll never find someone as good as me in Williamstown. Oh sure, maybe he won't have middle-age acne. But I'll haunt her for some time to come the way her memory haunts me. I can bolt upright in the night, guilty after dreaming that I took her back, even though in the dream I know it's wrong. I'm Swann with time on my hands to long for her and hate her at the same time.

Down at the roots of my turmoil lurk other models of truth, acknowledgment that I'd prepared myself for passion in the South Pacific, but didn't get lucky. I acknowledged that her values that I had dubbed daily as self-indulgence are harmless if not more valid in the current world. My real gripe lies in sensing that I'd be just as self-gratifying if I could. Far from wishing for our love to endure, I'd doubted it from the beginning. I intuited that she would exercise her free will better than I ever could, caught as I am in the myriad double-backs of runic Irish culture. In this time when I feel completely alone, I want to cling to her. But I would have cast her off frictionlessly the moment a new situation or lover materialized.

Of course, out of these self-damning possible truths, one occurred as a common reality: She dumped me before I could dump her. During the dissolution, I asked her if part of her loss of interest stemmed from my own loss of status, the Senior Editorship, the big bucks relative to her income. She admitted the possibility, though I thought then that she said so mostly as a manifestation of the healing balm of agreement applied by many women during such awful moments. Yet, more evidence of her characteristic drive for success heightened by her personal desire to break out of the second-class citizenship of being a girl-child, the sixth in a traditional Eastern European family, it made sense, it all made sense.

So, why did I stay with her so long, even when I had worked toward the end of the union from the start? The tenderness of her kiss, perhaps, the caress of lips upon lips. More likely, the reason resides in the comfort of companionship in my growing middle years. Or, it's told in the lines of a poem I wrote for her to send her on her way to Europe:

Ah, Marie!
When I think of
The curve of your
straight smile
gone beyond adult restraint,
and the sweetness
of your manner
to all who pass your door,
I'm bled dry
of malicious feeling,
I'm charmed.

Now, I hate all burnt-red Nissan Sentras, I hate France and the French, I hate San Francisco and her favorite son Matthew Wilder singing "Nobody gonna break my stride." And I sing songs, too, fantasizing about sending them to her: "You left me just when I needed you most." "Why don't you love me like you used to do?" and "Love has no pride." I'm all alone, now, with too much time knowing it.

So, you see, along with my loss of livelihood, my loss of self-confidence in my professional skills, I've also lost the frame of reference for hope. The slap in my face is that I'm thirty-five and no closer to the American Dream of family, home, career. Seeing my father distracted from dying by his children, I discovered that I want these distractions, too, fiercely. But I fear them as well, as investments of love that either will cause me the pain of separation by their deaths or their pain through mine. I see all of my little nephews and nieces and I quake thinking of car crashes, rapists, guns. They need to be protected, we all need to be protected, security.

My father once argued with my mother about the expense of sending all eight kids to school, that not all of us necessarily were college material. Mom said that in this day and age a college education was a weapon of survival and that she wasn't sending her kids out into the world with inferior weapons. The proof of this is that a kid I'd coached on a knee-high football team a decade ago, my favorite kid on the whole team, a feisty, enthusiastic little pest, was just picked up for cutting a man's throat. I knew ten years ago that he was a good kid in a lousy family. I blew my chance at Big Brotherhood, I let him get away. I told you the world has gone to shit.

I'll sing the song, if you want, "I really need this job." My career goal is to banish this reverberating despair from my life, and I need a socio/economic base to do it, to build up a new arsenal of life weapons. In exchange for such remuneration, I'll do anything you want. I await your reply with shortness of breath.

Sincerely,

Dennis J. McConaghy

Spitting fire, Yosemite Sam declares, "You mangy long-eared varmint, this town ain't big enough for the two of us."

Bugs runs off, and to the sound of hammers and nails, several skyscrapers pop up behind the wooden facade of the old western town called Rising Gorge.

"Now is it big enough?" asks Bugs.

"No it ain't, Rabbit!"

"Awright Sam," Bugs says, etching a line in the dust by dragging one foot in front of him. "Step across this line!"

"I'm a-steppin'!"

"This one!"

"I'm a-steppin'!"

"This one!"

Bugs watches as Sam drops off a cliff after crossing the last line.

282 South Street
Williamstown, PA
08102
February 8th, 1984

The Washington Post
Box No. M101
1150 15th Street, N.W.
Washington, D.C.
20071

Gentlefolk,

I read with keen interest your advertisement for a Public Relations/Technical Writer. I believe that my professional experience combined with my genuine desire to work on legislative issues for a nonprofit firm would enable me to bring special verve to this post. Hence, I would like to explore with you this employment opportunity toward our mutual benefit.

In Mr. Roger's Neighborhood, Earl the Pearl Monroe shows how to dribble a basketball. After feeding the fish, one shake, two shakes, Mr. Rogers changes his shoes and sweater. As he dons his jacket to leave, he sings "Tomorrow, tomorrow, we'll start the day tomorrow with a song or two."

Acknowledgments

Short stories seem straightforward enough—individuals deal with dilemmas that begin and end pretty quickly. Ideas for these stories often show up as stray thoughts, memories, or tiny "what-ifs" to be worked out like little puzzles or deductive logic. Compared to novels, they seem simple, yet enforce the same demands on their writers. Short stories need to present compelling tales, characters, and denouements like novels but on a much tinier canvas. To succeed, these miniatures must move readers to wish for more at story's end rather than to wish it ended halfway through. The hope to achieve good outcomes depends on engaging the best, honest editors and readers to critique every story before it leaves home. Those who have helped me through the past 50 years, for which I am deeply grateful, are listed below.

Lucie Brown, my sister and pal to whom this collection is dedicated, champions my stories enthusiastically. More importantly, she exercised her more than three decades as an elementary school teacher by copy editing my manuscripts to ensure that all is smooth and correct.

My brother George has read everything and always offers the best suggestions which I follow without second guessing as the right course.

Ivey, my lovely wife, the most amazing and accomplished editor I have ever known, read the stories and offered suggestions whenever I asked. Her brilliance comes from knowing when to lay it on me and when to lay off.

Jim O'Donnell has read everything as well. My best friend and chosen brother, never fails in supporting my efforts despite my spates of bad behavior.

Every one of my other family members read stories and encouraged me: my brother Pat, world class musician and writer in his own right; Lucie, my pal with the biggest of hearts who with crystal clarity knows what is and isn't important; Anne, fine artist and all-in altruist who always lifts us up; Ellen, wicked smart, true believer, and our unfailing bellwether of social justice. Finally, I offer my thanks and love to my daughter Molly and son Conor, who lead the way in progressive thinking, a great influence on their father.

About the Author

Dan Wallace worked in book publishing for 37 years, most of them at Gallaudet University Press. In 2014, he turned to writing full time. He has written five novels that include *Tribune of the People: A Novel of Ancient Rome* and *Run West: A Novel of the Civil War*. He has completed two other short story collections and also writes poetry and essays that can be read online at his writing exchange *In the Wallace Manner* (inthewallacemanner.com). He lives with his wife Ivey in the Washington, DC, area.

Mainstream Stories by Dan Wallace

A young West Virginia girl trained as a boxer by her father strikes up a troubling, long-distance friendship. Hoping to live the dream, a master plumber crosses the ocean to compete for a fantastic prize. In a small city museum, an ambitious curator crosses paths with two aspiring artists at an avant-garde exhibit. Humiliated after dropping a fly ball, a disillusioned boy's love of the game hinges on the actions of an old major leaguer. A young woman considering her tenth school reunion reminisces to decide.

These stories comprise an array that mine the country's cultural history during the past half century. Each offers vivid characterizations of common people and places as pieces in the puzzle of an ever-changing world. Insights abound in this wide-ranging collection well worth reading through and through.

Blossom Gold and other stories

By Dan Wallace

ISBN 978-1-7335725-6-9 trade paperback

ISBN 978-1-7335725-7-6 Kindle E-book

Wylisc Press, Silver Spring, MD

Available at Amazon.com

New Science Fiction Stories by Dan Wallace

Travel through space with provisional immortals as they panhandle for treasure amid a million iotas of galactic trash. Reserve a front-row seat for truly heroic Olympic feats performed on the Moon. Land on a desert planet where an eternal being chances the immolation of her gray matter forever. Follow a troubled blue-collar worker as he experiences an ultimate epiphany. Join an ambitious researcher who risks his own consciousness by delving into the depths of the permanently comatose. Track the progress of professional sports in ever-shifting environments.

Explore these and other alternate human prospects in this enriching, eclectic collection of stories. Each offers an original perspective on a broad spectrum of the probable and the possible. Together, they deliver an extraordinarily entertaining spectrum of what the future might hold.

Garbage in Space: Speculative Stories

By Dan Wallace

ISBN 978-1-7335725-8-3 trade paperback

ISBN 978-1-7335725-9-0 Kindle E-book

Wylisc Press, Silver Spring, MD

Now Available at Amazon.com

Novels by Dan Wallace

In the winter of 1861, East Tennessee mountain boy Billy McKinney finds himself marching with the Rebels to engage the Yankees at the Cumberland Gap. He never wanted to fight for the South because his preacher taught him that slavery was wrong. Mostly, though, Billy fears getting killed. In his first battle, he charges through a storm of gunfire and cannon shot amid a driving, icy rain. All around him his friends fall, their mouths bubbling bloody webs of agony. Terrified, Billy decides to run. In his mad dash, he meets up with four runaway slaves led by Bev Bowman. They take him along on their flight, though as prisoner or partner remains to be seen.

Run West is a compelling story of survival in a time of anguish and conflict that no one could escape.

Publishers Weekly—Wallace's epic novel triumphs with a vivid historical account of ambitious elite Roman politicians and generals.
Library Journal— This thoroughly researched novel is as dramatic and gory as any swords-and-sandals epic and demonstrates how educational historical fiction can be. A wide cast of characters including soldiers, senators, slaves, mothers, and wives expand the reader's understanding of life in this time.
Midwest Book Review—A deftly constructed, exceptionally well written, and consistently compelling read from beginning to end, "Tribune of the People" is a truly impressive novel of the old Roman Empire by Dan Wallace. This is the stuff from which block-buster movies are made!
The US Review of Books: Professional Book Reviews for the People— Wallace's epic tale vividly depicts the opulence and grandeur of the ruling classes while simultaneously detailing the sights, sounds, smells, and squalor of those not born to wealth or position. His battle scenes pulse with excitement as he couples the weapons, tactics, and strategies of war with the carnage they wreak. No less compellingly does he describe the deceit and scheming in the porticos of power as well as the intrigue and hidden agendas in intricate familial relationships. RECOMMENDED.
The Historical Novel Society—A most timely novel; the characters are engaging and well-formed and the story well told. The novel gives you a feel for ancient Rome in the last years of the Republic.

***Tribune of the People:* A Novel of Ancient Rome**

By Dan Wallace

ISBN 97917335725-0-7 trade paperback
ISBN 97817335725-1-4 Kindle E-Book
Wylisc Press, Silver Spring, MD

Available at Amazon.com

www.ingramcontent.com/pod-product-compliance
Lightning Source LLC
LaVergne TN
LVHW091147080826
845145LV00008B/2291

* 9 7 8 1 7 3 5 3 0 0 6 0 3 *